wondergirls™

The New Girl

Jillian Brooks

SCHOLASTIC INC.
New York Toronto London Auckland Sydney
Mexico City New Delhi Hong Kong

ISBN 0-439-35200-2

Copyright © 2002 17th Street Productions,
an Alloy Online, Inc. company.
All rights reserved.
Published by Scholastic Inc.

Produced by 17th Street Productions,
an Alloy Online, Inc. company
151 West 26th Street
New York, NY 10001

12 11 10 9 8 7 6 5 4 3 2   2 3 4 5 6/0

Printed in the U.S.A.   40
First Scholastic printing, January 2002

chapter
ONE

Hey, Felicia! We've already packed up our computer so I have to send this by regular mail. I still can't believe that in eight more days we'll both be living in Wonder Lake, IL! It's going to be so great. We'll be going to the same school, and we can hang out together all the time, just like we used to at the beach. My friends here in Charleston threw me an awesome going-away party last night. It was really hard to say good-bye to everyone, especially Chelsea (remember her?). But I'm actually kind of excited about moving. Like my dad says, it's going to be an adventure. I guess it's lucky that I make friends easily. And besides, I already know YOU! Well, I'd better keep packing or my mom's going to freak.

See you soon!
Love, Traci

"So, kids, what do you think?" my mom said. She turned around in the front seat of the minivan and gave me and my brother, Dave, a huge smile.

What did I think? Of my brand-new school in my brand-new town?

I stared at the huge stone building with the flag-pole out in front. It looked a lot bigger than it had in the Internet picture.

"Looks like a regular old school," Dave grumbled. "No big deal."

"Yeah, right," I muttered. Dave is thirteen, two years older than me. He was pretending to be cool, I could tell. But he kept rubbing his sweaty palms on his jeans. Total giveaway.

"Traci?" my mom asked. "Are you still with us?"

"Sure," I answered quickly. "Everything's going to be fine, Mom. Trust me."

I wanted to make my mom feel better. It was *her* first day at Wonder Lake Middle School, too. And she was probably a lot more nervous than Dave and I.

Mom's going to be the new music teacher at WLMS. They offered her the job when we were still living in South Carolina. We had to move because my dad's helping to set up the new medical center here. He's a pediatrician.

So were Dave and I lucky, or what? I mean, how many kids get the chance to go to school with their very own mom? *Every* day. *All* day.

Maybe that's what was making Dave sweat.

He reached for the car door handle.

"Hey, there's Patrick Bradley over there on the steps," he said. "Gotta go."

"Wait a minute, David," Mom said, frowning. "I haven't even parked the car yet. And who is Patrick Bradley?"

"He lives down the street, remember? We met him when we were moving in." Dave jumped out of the car and waved to us. "See you later!"

That left me all alone with good old Mom.

Don't get me wrong. She's a great mom, really. Most of the time. It was just, well . . . embarrassing, that's all. I didn't want to look like a total baby on my first day of sixth grade, walking in with my mother. Especially my mom the new *teacher*.

As she pulled into the faculty parking lot, my mom fumbled in her black tote bag for her lipstick. "Do I look okay?" she asked. "What about my hair? I didn't have time to blow-dry it this morning."

I looked at her reflection in the rearview mirror. Everyone says my mom and I look a lot alike. We both have light blond hair and brown eyes. So does Dave. Dad is a redhead.

"Mom, you look fine," I said.

"Thanks, honey," she said. "And you look very cute."

I glanced down at my white jeans and my favorite blue top. Cute? Not exactly the look I'd been going for.

3

"I mean, very cool," my mom corrected herself quickly.

I sighed. "Right," I said.

"Remember, Traci—positive attitude," Mom said. This time *she* was giving *me* the pep talk.

I gazed out the car window at all the kids heading into the school building. Mom is always telling me and Dave to keep a positive attitude. It drives us crazy. But I guess it's good advice.

I'd already decided I wasn't going to let anything get me down—today, anyway. For one thing, I'm an optimist. That means I always look on the bright side of everything. At least, I try to.

But here's the other reason: Today I was finally going to see my old friend Felicia Fiol again! She was starting sixth grade at Wonder Lake Middle School, too.

Felicia and I used to hang out together at the beach in the summers. She and her parents came to South Carolina on vacation every year. Until her parents got divorced.

Believe it or not, I hadn't seen Felicia for two whole years. We'd written letters sometimes and e-mailed each other, but that's never the same as talking in person. Would I even recognize her when I saw her?

My mom and I got out of the car. "I hope I find Felicia right away," I said. "It looks like a pretty big place."

Mom shaded her eyes against the early morning sun and squinted toward the huge building. "Well, it used to be a high school, so it *is* a lot bigger than your old school. But that also means it has excellent facilities. Anyway, I'm sure you and Felicia won't have any trouble finding each other."

I sure hoped not.

As we got closer to the school, it seemed to loom even larger. There were crowds of kids everywhere, chattering excitedly or just hanging around.

A blue sign with white-and-gold letters at the front of the building said: WONDER LAKE MIDDLE SCHOOL. HOME OF THE MUSKRATS.

Muskrats? Ugh. Don't get me wrong—I love furry animals of every kind. But it was hard to think of those scrawny little rodents being anyone's school mascot.

Back in Charleston, my soccer team would have been the Cooper River Panthers.

But I wasn't going to think about home right now. I was going to think about seeing Felicia.

Would she look exactly the same? Kind of tall and skinny, with waist-length, curly black hair and huge brown eyes? She always wore her hair in braids at the beach, and she was always the first one in the water, screaming at the top of her lungs as she jumped into the waves.

"Traci, honey, why don't you go on ahead?" my

mom said, breaking into my thoughts. We were halfway up the steps by now. "I need to stop at the office first."

"Okay," I said, totally relieved. "I'll be fine, really. Thanks." I couldn't wait to get inside.

"Good luck!" my mom called after me as I bounded up the rest of the steps.

I gave her a tiny wave over my shoulder as I rushed through the front doors. I had to find Felicia before the bell rang. Maybe we were even in the same homeroom.

But as I entered the lobby, I stopped short.

The inside of Wonder Lake Middle School looked like a huge cave. It was kind of dark, with stone walls and huge wooden beams overhead. I almost expected a bunch of bats to come flying out.

The place was packed with kids, talking and laughing. But I didn't see Felicia.

I looked around again. There were three long halls leading off the lobby. Which way should I go?

I quickly pulled out the schedule I'd gotten in the mail two days ago. Now I wished I'd gone to the orientation last week for sixth graders. But we hadn't moved yet.

Homeroom 201B.

I peered at the signs near the entrance of each hallway. BEAVER. FOX. BADGER. The names had little animal heads painted next to them. With beady, little eyes.

Well, that was helpful. No numbers. And two "B" names. Hmmm. Finding my homeroom might be trickier than I'd thought.

I quickly walked up to the nearest bunch of kids who looked like sixth graders.

Leaning against the wall next to a crowded trophy case was a girl wearing a purple tie-dyed shirt and flared jeans. She had long, straight brown hair parted in the middle. Beside her stood a pretty, auburn-haired girl, who was talking to some guy in cargo shorts and a neon orange T-shirt.

The second girl's outfit was perfect: a black sleeveless T-shirt with a splash of rhinestones and a short black denim skirt. Her hair was perfect, too. It hung just below her shoulders and was thick and shiny. And she was wearing makeup over her summer tan.

I cleared my throat. "Um, hi," I broke in. "Excuse me, but I'm new here. Can y'all tell me where I can find room 201B?"

The guy, who looked familiar, burst out laughing. "*Y'all?*" he hooted. "Hey, I think we've got ourselves a real live Dixie Chick here!"

Instantly, I felt my face flame red. Had I actually said "y'all"? And even if I had, was that some kind of crime in Wonder Lake?

The auburn-haired girl snickered loudly. Her hippie friend giggled and nudged her in the arm.

"Ryan thinks he's a total comedian," the hippie girl said.

"Right," I muttered, adjusting my knapsack a little tighter on my shoulder.

"None of us has a clue where room 201B is," the girl added.

"But if y'all want, we-all could help you find it," Ryan offered.

The auburn-haired girl punched him playfully. "Why, aren't you a real Southern gentleman?" she said, in an exaggerated drawl.

That made me really mad. Who did these kids think they were? "Never mind," I said huffily. Then I turned and stomped toward the nearest hallway. BEAVER, the sign said.

If I kept walking, maybe I'd just get lucky and my homeroom would magically appear.

"Yoo-hoo!" Ryan called after me, in a high-pitched voice. "See y'all later!"

I didn't turn around. I had to find Felicia—and fast. The three kids I'd just met weren't exactly friend material.

Not to sound conceited or anything, but I was pretty popular back at my old school. I'd known all my friends practically my whole life and never did anything without them.

But now, everything was different. For the first time in my life I felt like a complete outsider. And it was kind of a bad feeling.

chapter TWO

Have You Got the Right Stuff?
Coach Talbot Wants YOU!!!
Try Out for Wonder Lake Middle School's
Very Own State Champion
Girls' Soccer Team!
First Practice
Thursday, Sept. 13
2:45 SHARP
Soccer Field A
GO-O-O-O-O-O MUSKRATS!!!!!!!!

I pushed my way through the crowded hallway, trying to read the numbers on the doors and avoid being trampled at the same time.

I was looking out for Felicia, too, but all of the kids in the hall marked "Beaver" looked older than me.

Suddenly, I smacked right into Mom. She was standing in the middle of the hallway, frantically digging through her tote bag.

"Traci!" she said breathlessly when she saw me. "Am I glad to see you, honey! I can't find my schedule anywhere. And I just had it in my hand a minute ago, I'm sure of it."

A frizzy-haired girl in a Wonder Lake sweatshirt practically knocked me over with her tuba case as she passed.

This place was a total zoo. No wonder the halls had animal names.

"Uh, Mom? We're sort of in the middle of traffic here," I said.

Mom looked around. "Oh dear," she said. "You're right. Why don't we move over there by the lockers?"

It was so embarrassing. Kids were staring at us, I could tell. But what was I supposed to do?

My mom was getting pretty wound up now. "I know I'm supposed to be a homeroom teacher," she said, throwing up her hands. "I just don't know *which* homeroom."

"Maybe you should go back to the office and ask someone there," I suggested.

Mom sighed. "I suppose so," she said.

Luckily, the first bell rang right then. Saved!

"Sorry, Mom, gotta go. I don't know where my homeroom is, either. 201B."

My mom frowned. "201B? That does sound familiar. Maybe . . ."

But I was already halfway down the hall. "Bye!" I called back to Mom.

I finally found my classroom. It wasn't easy, let me

tell you. As it turned out, 201B is in Badger, not Beaver. That would be 201B*E*. Is that a dumb system, or what?

When I walked in, the second bell had already rung. That meant the teacher would mark me late on my very first day.

Except there was no teacher. Just a whole bunch of kids catching up on their summers and making tons of noise.

I looked around anxiously for Felicia, but there was no sign of her.

With a sigh, I headed toward one of the empty desks at the back of the room.

"Hey!" someone called. "Over here!"

I turned around. Felicia?

Not quite. To my surprise, it was Ms. Purple Tie-Dye from the lobby. She was sitting with her snooty friend Ms. Rhinestones and that clown Ryan.

I went over anyway. What did I have to lose?

"Hi, I'm Amanda Kepner," the girl said. "And this is Arielle Davis." She grinned. "You probably remember Ryan. Want to sit with us?"

"Sure," I said, taking the desk behind Amanda. "Thanks."

How come she was being so nice all of a sudden?

"Sorry if we were kind of rude before," Amanda said, as if she'd read my mind. "We're new at WLMS, too.

11

We got lost, too. I guess we weren't paying enough attention at orientation last week."

"Total waste of time," Arielle said. "You didn't miss a thing."

"So did you guys all go to the same school before?" I asked. That sounded dumb, but I wasn't sure what else to say.

Amanda shook her head. "Arielle and I have been friends since pre-K," she said. "She went to Wonder Lake Girls' Academy, and Ryan and I went to the lower school. But Arielle and I lived across the street from each other until she moved into a bigger house last year."

"I finally got my parents to let me go to a coed school," Arielle said, rolling her eyes. "It took *years* before they gave in."

"So where are y'all—I mean, *you*—from, anyway?" Ryan asked me. He was sitting on Amanda's desk, swinging his legs.

"South Carolaaahna," I said, drawing out the word. "Ever heard of it?"

Ryan just laughed. If he wasn't such a joker, he might have been cute, with his wild brown hair and brown eyes.

Amanda grinned at me. "Don't worry, you'll do just fine here at Wonder Lake. What's your name, anyway?"

"Traci McClintic," I said. I suddenly felt a little

shy. I'd never been "the new girl" before. It was harder than I thought it would be.

But Amanda seemed pretty nice, at least. I wasn't so sure about Arielle. She kept looking around the room while Amanda and I were talking. I definitely got the feeling I was butting in somehow. And that Arielle didn't like it.

"The teacher's still not here yet," she said, tossing her shiny hair. "We're off to a good start."

"So Traci, how long have you lived here?" Amanda asked.

"Since Friday," I told her. "Most of our stuff is still in boxes. I haven't even seen the town yet."

"My parents and I just moved, too," Arielle put in. I guess she'd been paying attention after all. "Into this really cool old mill. We just had the whole thing renovated. My mom's been working with a decorator from New York."

"That sounds nice," I said. I couldn't help glancing toward the door. Was Felicia ever going to show up?

I turned back to Arielle and Amanda. Ryan had jumped off Amanda's desk and was throwing a football around the back of the room with some other guys. "I have a really good friend who lives here in Wonder Lake," I said. "But I haven't seen her in two years."

Amanda raised her eyebrows. "Really? Who is she?"

"Felicia Fiol," I replied. "Do you know her?"

"The name sounds familiar," Amanda said slowly. "But I don't think so. She may have gone to one of the other elementary schools."

Arielle frowned. She was obviously thinking hard. "Felicia . . . her mom owns a bakery, right? I met her a couple of weeks ago, just before I left for soccer camp."

"Arielle knows practically everyone in town," Amanda told me.

Suddenly, a boy in the front of the room called out, "Teacher!"

Everyone scrambled for their seats and the room got quiet.

And then our homeroom teacher walked in.

My *mother*.

No! I thought wildly. *Not possible!*

"Hello, everyone," Mom said, smiling and looking around the room. I don't think she saw me in the back. "This *is* 201B, isn't it?"

"About time," Arielle muttered.

I put my head down on my desk. My life was over.

Amanda tapped me on the shoulder. "Hey, Traci, what's wrong? Are you okay?"

"I'm fine," I mumbled. "Just great."

"Well, I guess we'd better get started with the roll right away," Mom said brightly. She headed toward the desk. "I'm afraid we're a little behind schedule."

A boy on the other side of the room raised his hand. "When is lunch?" he asked.

My mom frowned. "Lunch?" she asked. "Goodness, I have no idea. But it's only eight-forty-five, young man. Didn't you have breakfast?"

I groaned. Mom wasn't going to start on her "importance of a well-balanced breakfast" speech, was she? Dave and I heard it almost every morning. But this was *school*.

Fortunately, my mom seemed a little distracted. She turned away from the desk and wrote her name on the blackboard in large, flowing script.

I sank lower in my seat.

"As you can see, my name is Ms. McClintic," Mom announced.

Am I supposed to call her that? I wondered. Maybe I could get transferred to another homeroom.

Or better yet, to another planet.

"I teach music classes, and I'll also be directing the marching band and orchestra," Mom went on.

Arielle rolled her eyes. "Lame," she whispered.

I frowned. This girl was really starting to get on my nerves.

Mom brushed back a stray wisp of blond hair. "Now let's see, where *is* that roll book? I just saw it...."

A girl wearing glasses and a red kerchief in her

hair cleared her throat. "It's, um, on your desk, Ms. McClintic," she said, pointing.

I really felt sorry for Mom. Her morning wasn't going much better than mine.

But I knew things were going to look up.

They just *had* to.

Roll call seemed to take forever. I found out that Ryan's last name was Bradley. That's where I'd seen him before; he was Patrick Bradley's younger brother—my new neighbor.

I braced myself as Mom headed toward the M's.

Sure enough, she looked up from the roll book and beamed. "Oh, there you are, Traci," she said. "Way in the back of the room. I guess we both found our homerooms after all."

I scrunched down in my chair and cringed. I could feel everyone staring at me.

"She *knows* you?" Arielle whispered.

Just then, a tiny, folded-up piece of paper landed on my desk.

I practically pounced on the note. *Traci, want to have lunch with us? A.*

Well, "A." sure wasn't Arielle. It had to be Amanda. She was smiling over her shoulder at me. Arielle, on the other hand, was definitely glaring at me. What was her problem?

I scrawled back, *Thanks, I'd love to. But I'll probably eat with Felicia. (If I find her!)* Then I folded up the paper and, with a quick glance at the front of the room, passed it back to Amanda.

I didn't want to get busted by my own mom for passing notes. Talk about humiliating.

Amanda wrote something back. Then, without turning around, she flipped the note over her shoulder. It landed on target, right in the middle of my desk.

Why don't all of us eat together?

Sure, why not? Amanda was definitely going out of her way to be nice.

Unlike some other people. I could swear I saw Arielle shaking her head "no" at Amanda.

But Amanda just shrugged and ignored her.

When the bell finally rang for first period, I was out of homeroom like a shot. I hardly said good-bye to Amanda. And I didn't dare look back at my mom.

But I heard Arielle's voice behind me say, "Is Ms. McClintic a major flake or what?"

My ears burned. Did Arielle mean my mom—or me? Either way, I'd definitely had enough of her.

I looked down at my already crumpled schedule and headed toward the hall with the sign that said FOX with a little fox head on it.

I was sure the animal eyes were watching me.

All I could do was hope that Felicia had first period in Fox hall, too. Something had to go my way that morning—it just had to.

chapter
THREE

```
Welcome WLMS Students!

Menu:
Wednesday, Sept. 12:
Cheesy Noodle Surprise
celery and carrot sticks
milk or juice
assorted fresh fruits
baked potato crisps
choice of yogurt or Jell-O

Have a Happy and Healthy School Year!
```

ARIELLE'S SAVING SEATS BY THE WINDOWS. SEE YA THERE AMANDA.

"Hey, is this the way to the cafeteria?" I asked a boy walking beside me in the hall.

He nodded. "Yep. Just follow the crowd."

I still hadn't seen Felicia yet. But I spotted my brother, Dave, heading down the hall in the other direction. I waved, but he didn't see me. He was deep in conversation with some guy in a NASCAR T-shirt.

Lucky Dave had already found a new friend—he's really into car racing.

Mom was there, too. She was taping a poster on the music room door about orchestra tryouts next week. And I *was* going to stop and say hi. Honest. But the crowd was sweeping me along too quickly toward the cafeteria.

All the sixth graders were supposed to eat at the same time. That meant I *had* to see Felicia. Finally!

The cafeteria, unlike the rest of the school, was bright and sunny. It had huge windows along three sides, like a giant greenhouse. Amanda had said a table "by the windows." But which windows?

I went quickly through the cafeteria line and grabbed a plate of gross-looking Cheesy Surprise. School food was definitely the same everywhere. Then I headed toward the farthest part of the room with my tray. I'd just have to work my way down until I found Amanda and Arielle.

As it turned out, that wasn't too hard. The two of them were laughing and talking, surrounded by a whole group of kids.

Maybe I should go sit somewhere else, I told myself. Amanda and Arielle already had plenty of people at their table.

Oh, go on, I said to myself. *What are you afraid of?*

As I started toward the table, Amanda saw me and waved. "There's lots of room," she called.

Arielle looked up and scowled.

She hardly moved over one inch to let me sit down.

"Hey, we were just leaving," one of the girls at the table said quickly. "There's a sign-up sheet for Pep Club outside the gym. We have to put our names down."

"See you guys later," Arielle called after them. Then she gave me an annoyed look, as if I'd interrupted something important.

"So, Traci, how's it going?" Amanda asked me. "I keep getting lost—what about you?"

I punched a hole in the top of my chocolate milk with a straw. "About every ten seconds," I said.

Arielle shrugged. "It's not so bad," she said. "Soon this place will seem like kindergarten. Trust me."

I wanted to think that Arielle was trying to make me feel better. But somehow what she'd said made me feel like a little kid.

Stop being paranoid, I told myself. *As soon as Felicia shows up, you can leave.* I kept one eye on the lunch line.

Arielle turned back to Amanda. "So anyway, I was talking to some of the girls from the team after English. They all think I've got a really good chance of making cuts, even as a sixth grader. First practice is tomorrow, and I definitely want to impress Coach Talbot."

Now Amanda turned to me. It was like having a

translator or something. "Arielle went to sleep-away soccer camp this summer," she said. "She's a really amazing player."

Arielle stirred her yogurt with a plastic spoon. "No big deal," she said, in an offhand way.

I leaned eagerly across the table. "Hey, guess what? I play soccer, too," I said. "My friend Chelsea and I went to AYSO soccer camp for a week in August."

Arielle didn't seem impressed. "Oh, AYSO," she said. But she made it sound like, "Oh, please."

"What's AYSO?" Amanda asked.

"It stands for 'American Youth Soccer Organization,'" I told her. I looked straight at Arielle. "And it's just as good as some fancy private school league."

I knew I shouldn't have said that. But I couldn't help it. Arielle was the biggest snob I'd ever met.

"Making the soccer team here in Wonder Lake is pretty tough, you know," Arielle said. "We're state champions."

We? That really bugged me. I mean, Arielle wasn't even on the team yet.

"I play center forward," I said.

Arielle raised her brows. "Really?" she said. "That's my position, too."

Well, at least Arielle and I had *something* in common.

"Listen, Traci. Don't feel bad if you don't make

22

cuts," Arielle went on. "They'll probably put you on sixth-grade JV. And there's always Pep Club. Why don't you go sign up? They take everybody."

My mouth dropped open. Was this girl for real? She was so incredibly rude. How could Amanda stand hanging out with her?

Amanda gave Arielle a warning look. "Whatever," Amanda said. Then, to change the subject, she added quickly, "Hey, did you guys get through all the books on the summer reading list?"

"Oh, sure," Arielle said, waving her spoon. "My parents made sure of that. I couldn't go to soccer camp until I'd finished ten books. Boooooring."

"I thought they were all pretty good," Amanda said. "I even did a few of the extra-credit reports."

"I read a really interesting book about Alaska," I offered, taking a bite of my Cheesy Surprise. "There were all these sled dogs in it and—"

"Dogs? Arrrrf, arrrf!"

I didn't even have to turn around. It was Ryan Bradley, passing behind me with his tray.

"Ignore him," Amanda advised under her breath.

"Aren't dog books kind of . . . babyish?" Arielle asked me.

"Hey, wait a minute! I like animals, too," Amanda put in quickly. She glanced at me with a worried frown.

But right then it didn't bother me that Arielle was

23

being such a pain. I'd just spotted Felicia, coming out of the lunch line!

I stood up and waved my arms over my head. "Felicia!" I called loudly.

The whole cafeteria was probably staring at me. But I was so glad I'd found my old friend, I didn't care.

Felicia kind of jumped a little. But then she beamed her great big smile and hurried over to the table.

"Hey, wait a minute," Amanda said. "I *do* know that girl. She was in my class last year. She's really shy and quiet."

Huh? Felicia, shy? Those summers in Charleston she was always really fun and outgoing.

I got up and went over to meet Felicia halfway. I wanted to give her a big hug, but I couldn't. She was holding a tray of Cheesy Surprise.

So I just stood there, smiling. "Hey, Felicia," I said, feeling a tiny bit awkward. This wasn't exactly how I'd pictured our big reunion.

"Hi, Traci," Felicia said, smiling back. "You look exactly the same."

I guess that was probably true. But Felicia looked totally different. Not like I thought she would, anyway. She was taller and her curly dark hair was cut to just below her shoulders. She was wearing a black miniskirt and a cool striped tank top. She seemed . . . more grown-up, somehow.

"Well, come on," I said. "We have a seat saved for you."

Felicia followed behind me, but I thought I'd seen a funny look cross her face. What was wrong?

"Who are you sitting with?" Felicia asked.

"Amanda Kepner and Arielle Davis," I said. "Arielle says she knows you. And Amanda was in your class last year."

"Arielle remembers me?" Felicia said. "Wow, that's great!"

I turned around to stare at her. Why was that so great?

"I mean, Arielle's really popular and all," Felicia said. "I can't believe she even remembers my name."

By then we'd arrived at the table. "Hi," Felicia said shyly to Amanda and Arielle.

"Oh, hi, Felicia," Arielle said. "Have a seat."

Felicia eagerly put her tray down on the other side of Arielle's.

Was I crazy, or did Felicia seem happier to see Arielle than she was to see me?

You're being paranoid, I told myself.

"So how did you guys know each other?" Amanda asked me.

"How was the rest of your summer?" Arielle asked Felicia, at the same time.

"Well, we were at the beach, standing next to each other at the snack bar," I answered. "And Felicia was holding this tiny little dog. It tried to lick my ice cream cone. Then the whole scoop fell into Felicia's french fries and . . ." My voice trailed off.

Felicia wasn't even listening. Arielle was telling her all about her fancy soccer camp.

"That must have been funny," Amanda said to me.

"Yeah, it was," I answered, staring down at my hardened Cheesy Surprise. I forced myself to take a few more bites, so I wouldn't have to talk anymore.

I couldn't believe it. Felicia seemed to be hanging on Arielle's every word!

Then I heard Arielle say, "You are *so* lucky you don't have McClintic for homeroom. Major space case. I bet she'll quit in two weeks. You should have seen her this morning. She—"

I just sat there, frozen in my chair.

Amanda cleared her throat. "Uh, Arielle . . ."

But Arielle paid no attention. "She'd probably lose her head if it wasn't attached to her body," she went on.

That was enough. I jumped to my feet, my face hot. "That happens to be my *mom* you're talking about, Arielle."

Arielle stopped in mid-sentence. Her mouth was actually hanging open. And she looked totally embarrassed.

Felicia just looked horrified—and really nervous. She kept glancing from me to Arielle.

"Sorry, Traci," Arielle said. But she didn't *look* very sorry. She shrugged. "How was I supposed to know she was your mom? I mean, you didn't say anything."

"Traci told us her name, Arielle," Amanda said. "Remember?" Then she pointed to the big loose-leaf notebook beside my tray. I'd written "Traci Ann McClintic" across the front, in huge letters.

"Oh. Sorry," Arielle said again. Felicia looked relieved.

I felt kind of stupid now. I sat back down in my chair. Now what?

For a couple of seconds, no one said anything.

I figured it was up to me to get things going again. "So, Felicia," I said. "What are you doing after school?"

"I'm going to my dad's," Felicia said quietly. "He runs an animal shelter now. It's attached to our house. I usually help him out after school."

"Wow!" I said. "I thought your dad worked at the bakery."

Felicia shrugged and started biting her pinky nail. Last time I saw her she said she'd quit doing that. I guess she picked it up again. "Well, he used to. Didn't I tell you the whole story in one of my e-mails?"

"I don't think so," I said. "I'm sure I would have remembered."

"Well, Dad's still a part-owner of the bakery with

my mom. But he's always been into helping animals. And Wonder Lake needed its own shelter, so . . ."

"Hey, that's great!" I said. "Can I visit sometime?"

"Sure," Felicia said. "You can come home with me today after school, if you want."

I nodded eagerly. That sounded awesome.

"Wait a minute, Felicia. I thought you told me you lived above the bakery," Arielle said, frowning.

"Well, I do," Felicia said, looking flustered. "I mean, on weekends. That's when I'm with my mom. But she has to get up at three in the morning to start the ovens, so I spend school nights with my dad."

"Three A.M.? Ugh." Arielle shuddered.

"That's pretty cool, working at night," Amanda said. "And your mom's croissants are the best."

Felicia smiled shyly. "Hey, do you and Arielle want to come to the shelter this afternoon, too?" she asked Amanda.

"Well, I definitely want to come," Amanda said. She turned to Arielle. "Going to the shelter sounds like fun, don't you think?"

"Sure," Arielle said, looking bored. "Count me in, too."

Felicia's eyes lit up. She looked completely thrilled. But Arielle was already glancing over her shoulder at some guy from our English class.

I couldn't help being a little disappointed that it wasn't going to be just me and Felicia hanging out

28

together after school. We needed to catch up on things. Get to know each other again.

Because to tell you the truth, Felicia seemed a lot different than I remembered. Sort of shy and nervous. And hanging on Arielle's every word.

I just didn't get it. Could she really have changed so much in two years?

chapter
FOUR

Notes passed in math class:

F: Can't wait until after school! Math is the WORST!-T

T: At least we're in the same class! i Wish your mom was our teacher instead of lame Mr. Reid. Did you see him clipping his nails while we were copying that stuff from the board? Gross. Meet me outside Room 203-Beaver at last bell.-F

F: What's the difference between a Beaver and a Badger, anyway?-T

T: No clue!-F

"Bus passes, please, ladies," the driver said as Felicia, Arielle, Amanda, and I boarded the school bus for Felicia's neighborhood.

"Um, I don't have one yet," I told him. My mom was probably planning to drive me and Dave to school forever.

The driver shrugged. "Sorry," he said. "But those are the rules. No pass, no ride."

"Please let Traci on, sir," Arielle said. She smiled at the driver. "She's new here in Wonder Lake."

I felt myself flush with embarrassment. Everyone on the bus was staring at me.

"Well, all right, if she's a friend of yours," the driver said. He smiled back at Arielle. "But don't forget next time, okay?" he added to me.

"I won't," I promised. Then I went to sit with Felicia behind Amanda and Arielle.

"Thanks," I whispered to Arielle.

This time she actually smiled at me. "No problem," she said. "You can owe me."

Why did I have a feeling she wasn't kidding?

"So where do you live, Traci?" Amanda asked, twisting in her seat.

"We're renting a place on East Lake Road," I said. "Where *is* Wonder Lake, anyway? I haven't seen it yet."

Arielle and Amanda exchanged glances. Then Arielle giggled. What was so funny?

"Oh, you'll find out," she said. "It's really close to your house, actually."

"My dad is going to be so surprised to see you, Traci," Felicia said. "I didn't have a chance to tell him you were living here yet."

She didn't even tell her parents? I guess my moving

32

to Wonder Lake wasn't as big a deal to Felicia as it was to me.

Arielle turned around. "Hey, guess what? I'm having a huge back-to-school party," she said. loudly enough for everyone on the bus to hear.

"Really?" Felicia said eagerly. "When?"

"In two weeks," Arielle said. "My parents *finally* said yes. I had to work on them all summer. The renovations are all done on our house now, so it's the perfect time."

"Did someone say party?" a kid across the aisle asked.

Arielle started telling half the bus about her big party plans. "We're going to have a DJ and everything," she said.

I couldn't help hoping I'd be invited, too. It sounded like fun. But I wasn't so sure Arielle liked me enough to invite me.

"Hey, a party will be a great way for you to meet everyone," Amanda told me. She glanced at Felicia. "You guys will both come, right?"

"Sure," Felicia said hastily. "We'll be there."

"Definitely," I promised.

I was feeling a little better now. I'd finally found Felicia, and I'd made friends with Amanda. Even Arielle seemed to be warming up a little. My first day at Wonder Lake Middle School had actually turned out okay. Except maybe for the Mom part.

We reached Felicia's stop about fifteen minutes later. She and her dad lived way out on the edge of town. I guess Mr. Fiol needed more space for all the animals.

"This is it," Felicia announced when the bus dropped us off. We started walking up a long, dirt driveway. "Wonder Lake's first animal shelter."

At first I didn't see anything at all. Then I spotted a small, white farmhouse with a screened porch at the top of the driveway. There was a blue van parked under a tree, and I could hear lots of barking from somewhere.

"Most of the animals are out back," Felicia told us. "Sometimes we keep a few in the house, especially if they're injured. A vet comes by on Tuesdays and Thursdays and for emergencies."

Just then, a tall, dark-haired man in a plaid shirt came around the side of the house. I recognized Felicia's dad right away. He was wearing work gloves and carrying a bucket.

"Well, what have we here?" Mr. Fiol's voice boomed. "Did I just acquire a few extra daughters?"

"Dad!" Felicia protested. She glanced at Arielle as though she were completely embarrassed.

"Traci McClintic, is that you?" Mr. Fiol came up and gave me a huge bear hug. "What are you doing here? I didn't know you were planning a visit."

"I, um, live here now," I said. "As of last week."

34

Mr. Fiol cocked his head. "Well, isn't that something?" he said. "You and your folks certainly are a long way from Charleston."

That's for sure, I thought.

"Dad," Felicia said, tugging on his sleeve. "This is Arielle Davis. And Amanda Kepner. They're friends of mine from school. They came to see the shelter."

"Well, that's wonderful," Mr. Fiol said. "Why don't I give all you girls a tour?"

"Thanks, Mr. Fiol," I said. "That'd be great."

Felicia and her dad took us around to the back of the house. The shelter was kind of like a small barn with wooden cages leading into outside runs. It wasn't painted or anything, and it looked kind of rough, but Mr. Fiol seemed very proud of it. "We're still getting set up," he explained. "But we've made a lot of progress and the animals seem right at home."

Out back, the runs were filled with dogs, cats, chickens, and rabbits. There were animals *everywhere*. The yard was muddy and the grass had been torn up in places. Beside the house was an old-fashioned water pump.

Arielle hugged her arms close to her chest. "It smells back here," I heard her whisper to Amanda.

"Shhh," Amanda told her.

"It's getting a little crowded, as you can see," Mr. Fiol went on. "New animals come in every day. Big and small, young and old, sick and healthy—we take them all."

"You don't put any of them to sleep, do you?" Arielle asked.

Mr. Fiol shook his head. "No," he said. "And I sure hope we can keep it that way. Like I said, we're pretty tight on space here."

I felt sorry for the poor animals. But they all seemed happy and well cared for. And at least they had a place to go while they were waiting to be adopted.

"Hey, Buster," Mr. Fiol said sharply. "Cut that out!" A little black-and-white dog had wriggled under the fence and was poking his nose in a cat's litter pan.

"Gross," Felicia said, glancing at Arielle.

She seemed pretty squeamish for a girl who was used to being around animals.

"Oh, look, a duck pond!" Arielle said, pointing beyond the pens. "Can we go see it?"

"Sure," Felicia said eagerly. "I'll take you over. We can feed the ducks if you want. Come on, I'll go get some feed."

The two of them headed over to a group of large metal cans lined up outside the shelter.

Amanda and I walked toward the front of the house again with Mr. Fiol.

"Do you have any pets, Traci?" Amanda asked. "I

have two really fat, spoiled cats. They're my step-mom's, so now they live with us."

"I wish I could have pets," I said with a sigh. "But my brother, Dave, has major allergies. He can't be around animals, flowers, weeds, dust, or mildew. Practically the only place he doesn't sneeze is in the middle of the ocean. I used to go to this one pet store in Charleston all the time just so I could pet the animals."

"Gee, that's too bad," Amanda said sympathetically.

Suddenly, there was a loud honk from a mail truck pulling up the driveway.

Mr. Fiol jogged toward it. "Hey, Carter!" he called to the driver. "Do you have my letter today?"

"Sure do!" the postal carrier called back, pulling the truck to a stop. "State of Illinois Department of Animal Welfare. Would that be the one?"

He handed Mr. Fiol an envelope.

"This is it, all right," Mr. Fiol replied, holding up a long white envelope. "Thanks a lot, Carter."

The mail carrier waved good-bye and headed back down the driveway in his truck, just as Felicia and Arielle came back.

"Keep your fingers crossed, girls," Mr. Fiol said, tapping the envelope.

"It's a grant," Felicia whispered to us. "Dad's try-ing to raise money to expand the shelter. He's hoping for a really big check."

All of us gathered around Felicia's dad. He opened the letter and read it quickly.

A frown crossed his face.

"What is it, Dad?" Felicia asked. She sounded worried. "Are they going to give you the money?"

Mr. Fiol sighed. "I'm afraid not," he said. "Not enough, anyway. The state is only offering me a quarter of what I asked for."

"But that's so unfair!" I said. "Don't they want you to help all these poor animals?"

"Well, of course they do, Traci," Mr. Fiol said. "But there isn't enough money to go around. I was hoping to buy more food and supplies and hire some part-time help. I have a few volunteers, but . . ." He shook his head sadly. "I only have enough food for all these animals to last another ten days or so."

"Wait a minute!" I said. "I can help after school sometimes."

"Me too," Amanda said. "When I don't have to baby-sit my little brothers and sisters, anyway."

"Well, thank you, girls," Felicia's dad said. "We sure could use an extra hand or two. It's very nice of you to offer."

"Are there any other places you can ask for money?" Amanda asked.

Mr. Fiol shook his head. "I've pretty much asked every animal organization and agency I could find," he said. "I guess I'll have to figure out another way to come up with the money."

"Back in Charleston, we had car washes to raise money for our soccer team," I said.

Mr. Fiol smiled. "That's a good idea, Traci. But I think we might need something a little bigger to keep this shelter going. And I'm afraid we don't have much time."

Amanda seemed to be thinking hard. "What about that fund-raiser they had last spring for the library? They raised enough money to add a whole new wing, and all they did was have a barbecue and give away some books."

Mr. Fiol raised his eyebrows.

"You could have a fund-raiser just like that one on the village green next weekend," Amanda said. "And we could help you get the word out around school."

"And all over town," I added, catching on to her idea. "I bet if we put up posters and made phone calls and everything . . ."

Mr. Fiol held up one hand. "Whoa, wait a minute," he began.

"We could call the fund-raiser 'All For Paws,'" I went on excitedly. That was the name of my favorite pet store back in Charleston.

"That's a great name," Amanda said, just as eagerly. She looked back at Arielle and Felicia. "Don't you think?"

They both nodded, although neither of them looked all that thrilled about the idea.

"Next Saturday doesn't leave us much time," Mr. Fiol said doubtfully.

"But you only have enough food for another week or two," Amanda pointed out. "We don't *have* any more time."

"We can do it," I said confidently. I looked around at Amanda, Arielle, and Felicia for their support.

Amanda nodded immediately. Felicia bit her pinky fingernail, waiting to see what Arielle would do. Arielle hesitated for another second. Then she nodded, too.

"See?" I cried. "It's all set!"

"Don't worry, Mr. Fiol," Amanda said. She shrugged off her knapsack and pulled out a spiral notebook. "We'll help you cover every detail."

"And when Amanda says that, she means it," Arielle added. "She's super-organized."

"Please, Dad?" Felicia said.

Mr. Fiol gave us a huge smile. "How can I resist a team like this?"

Soon we were all talking at once, making plans for the fund-raiser. "The first thing we'll need is a town permit to hold an event on the green," Mr. Fiol said.

Amanda began firing questions at Mr. Fiol and taking notes. "What kind of budget can we work with?" she said. "That's the best place to start."

But after a few minutes, Arielle looked bored. "I'm really thirsty," she told Felicia.

"Hey, does anyone want a soda?" Felicia asked quickly. "I'll run into the house and get some."

"Thanks," Arielle said. "I'll go with you."

I frowned over my shoulder as the two of them walked off together. It didn't seem like Arielle was very interested in helping us with the fund-raiser. But I was so excited about the whole idea that I didn't really care.

And then the best thing happened. This really adorable St. Bernard puppy came bounding up to me. She was huge—brown and white, with the most enormous paws I'd ever seen.

She drooled a lot, too. But I thought she was the cutest dog I'd ever laid eyes on. I'd already fallen completely in love with her.

Mr. Fiol laughed. "Traci, meet Lola," he said. "Lola, calm down! These girls are our guests."

I let Lola lick my face. "She's so friendly," I said. "Is she your dog?"

Mr. Fiol shook his head. "No," he said. "We're trying to find a good home for that pup. But so far, we haven't had any takers."

"Maybe we can find someone to adopt her at the fund-raiser," Amanda said.

"I sure hope so," Mr. Fiol said, sounding a little sad again. "Feeding Lola is like feeding three dogs in one."

Felicia and Arielle came out of the house with a

pitcher of lemonade. I drank mine with Lola in my lap as we all talked about the fund-raiser some more.

Before I knew it, my mom drove up the driveway to pick me up.

I thanked Mr. Fiol and said good-bye to everyone. Lola followed me all the way to the car.

"Don't worry, cutie-pie," I whispered into her fluffy puppy ear. "I can't adopt you because of my dork brother's allergies. But I promise we'll find you the best home ever by next Saturday."

chapter
FIVE

Note on McClintics' fridge:

Kids—
Had to leave early for faculty meeting.
Picked up bus passes from the office
yesterday—they're on the counter. Don't
even THINK of skipping breakfast—
blueberry waffle batter on stove. Traci:
Knock 'em dead this afternoon!
Love, Mom

"We have to cook our own breakfast?" Dave said. He was standing in the kitchen in his pajamas, frowning at the note Mom had left us on the fridge. "Bummer."

I rolled my eyes. "Deal with it," I said, pouring some cereal into a bowl.

"Your mom can't do everything around here, you know," Dad said. He was already dressed for work in khakis and a shirt and tie, sipping coffee.

"Hey, look on the bright side," I told my brother. "We get to take the bus."

Dad glanced at his watch. "And it will be here in ten minutes," he said. "Better get moving."

Dave grumbled all the way up the stairs.

I pushed my cereal around in my milk. I didn't really feel like eating anything. My stomach was kind of queasy.

"What's the matter, Traci?" Dad asked. "You're usually in such a hurry to get to school."

"I know," I sighed. "I'm just deciding whether or not to try out for the soccer team today."

"Well, why wouldn't you?" Dad said. He looked surprised. "You were the star of your team last season."

"That was back in Charleston," I said. "It's different here."

"It can't be that much different," Dad said. He picked up his briefcase and came over to kiss me goodbye. "Just do your best and you can't go wrong."

"Right," I said. "Thanks, Dad."

He smiled. "Chin up, Traci," he said cheerfully. Then he headed out the door to his car.

I thought about the soccer tryouts all the way to school. No one on the bus was paying any attention to me, anyway; they were busy throwing some poor kid's lunch around.

Did I want to be a Muskrat? I asked myself.

Of course I did. So what was the problem?

44

I knew the answer to that one.

Arielle.

I looked down at my black gym bag on the seat beside me, with my old Panthers patch sewn onto it. *Oh, who cares about Arielle Davis?* I thought. *It's up to the coach to decide who makes the team.*

I slid into homeroom just as Mom was closing the door. "Did you eat breakfast?" she whispered as I walked in.

"*Yes,*" I hissed, hoping no one had heard her.

I hurried to my seat behind Amanda. She smiled at me as I passed her desk.

Arielle was sitting next to Amanda. She gave me a little wave over her shoulder, but she didn't turn around.

"Good morning, everyone," Mom said. "Before we do the roll, I have a list of today's announcements from the office."

A few kids groaned.

Mom began to read from a bulletin. "The first meeting of the newspaper staff will be held at two-thirty in room 315F."

Then Mom looked up and smiled straight at me. "I know this next one will interest some of you. The first girls' soccer practice is also today after school. All returning Muskrats should report to Field A at two-forty-five. Girls who wish to try out for the team must sign up beforehand on the list posted outside of the locker room."

Arielle whirled around in her seat. "Did you sign up?" she asked me.

"Not yet," I said. "But I'm going to. Did you?"

"Of course," Arielle replied, flipping her hair. "I'm first on the list."

By now Mom had moved on to Student Behavior in the Lunchroom. But no one was really paying attention.

Amanda turned around. "I'm sure you'll both do great," she said to me and Arielle.

Arielle just kind of smiled and shrugged. "Hey, a little competition never hurts. Right, Traci?"

But the way she said it, it was more like, "You're no competition for me at all."

What made Arielle so sure of that? I mean, even my brother admits I'm a pretty decent soccer player. I *was*, anyway. Back in Charleston.

Would things be different here in Wonder Lake?

Were Muskrats tougher than Panthers?

I was about to find out.

Arielle and I walked down to the field house together after school.

"Today will be a piece of cake," she said. "Just some easy drills. After first cuts it gets a lot harder."

"Right," I mumbled.

The locker room was old and dark, with wooden lockers. It was actually kind of cool, although it smelled pretty musty.

"Hey, Arielle, good luck," some girl called on her way to the weight room.

I didn't let that bother me. So what if everyone knew Arielle? Then Arielle pulled on Muskrat colors: blue shorts with a blue-and-white soccer shirt. "It's signed by every player on the U.S. National Women's Team," she told me. "Cool, huh? My dad got it for me."

"That's great," I said. I looked down at my plain gray sweatshirt. Not exactly flashy.

Arielle even had blue laces and a gold scrunchie for her hair. What was this, a fashion show?

My cleats looked really old and dirty. I tried to scrape some of the dried mud off against one of the bench legs without much success. Luckily, Arielle didn't seem to notice. She was too busy adjusting her perfect ponytail.

"Okay, ladies, listen up!" a voice called. It was Coach Talbot. No doubt about it. She was six feet tall, with curly red hair and a sunburned nose. She was carrying a clipboard and wore a big silver whistle on a blue-and-white rope around her neck.

"Welcome to our first preseason Muskrats practice," Coach Talbot went on. "I should have all of your names on the sign-up sheet. Am I missing anyone?"

I half raised my hand. "Um, me," I said. "Sorry, I forgot to sign up." Boy, did I feel dumb.

Coach Talbot squinted across the room. "And you are . . . ?"

"Traci McClintic," I answered. For some reason, Coach Talbot was making me even more nervous. I felt as if her bulging blue eyes were boring into me.

"Who have you played for? The Lightnings? Wizards? How long?"

"AYSO," I said. "In South Carolina. Three years."

Coach Talbot shrugged. "Okay, McClintic, you're in Group B," she said, jotting something down on her clipboard. Then she turned back to everyone else. "When we hit the field, I'll call out the rest of the group assignments. Then we'll go through a few basic drills. Got it?"

Everyone nodded. Arielle gave Coach Talbot the same smile she'd given the bus driver yesterday.

I almost threw up when Coach Talbot smiled back.

"Arielle Davis, right?" she said. "I saw you play against St. Luke's Prep this summer. Glad to have you with us."

It sounded like Arielle had a good reason for being so smug. She probably had these tryouts in the bag already.

Stop it, I told myself. *Positive attitude, remember?*

So what if Arielle made the team? There were only a few spots open. There wasn't room for everyone.

Except I *knew* I deserved a place on the team, too.

Of course Arielle was in Group B with me. And I had to give her credit. She was good. Really good.

But I did okay, too. The first few passing drills were easy. I didn't mess up once, even when I was paired with Arielle. Then Coach Talbot had us do laps around the field.

As I passed in front of one of the goalposts, puffing a little, I heard someone call my name.

"Way to go, Traci!"

It was Felicia, and Amanda was with her. The two of them were waving at me.

"Break a leg, Traci!" Amanda called.

For just a second, I broke my stride. Then I felt a sudden rush of wind behind me.

I'm not sure exactly how it happened, but somehow I tripped. And Arielle fell, too—right over me.

I think I got the wind knocked out of me, because I couldn't breathe for a minute, and I felt dizzy.

The next thing I knew, Felicia and Amanda were standing over us.

"Are you guys okay?" Amanda asked, sounding really worried.

Felicia looked horrified. "Oh my gosh," she said.

Coach Talbot and the other girls from the team were already running over.

"I'm fine," I said, getting to my feet.

But Arielle didn't get up. She was sitting on the track with her hands over her face.

"Arielle, what's wrong?" Amanda asked.

"Make way, please, ladies," Coach Talbot said. She

knelt down beside Arielle and examined her face. She shook her head.

"Looks like you're going to have a pretty nasty shiner, Davis," she said. "You must have gotten an elbow in the eye. We'll need to get some ice on that right away."

Arielle nodded and turned away. I could see that her eye was already puffing up and turning purple.

Had I really done that?

I didn't mean to, of course. But I felt terrible. "I'm really, really sorry, Arielle," I said. "It was an accident."

"Of course it was," Coach Talbot said briskly.

But Arielle didn't answer.

Felicia had already run to the bleachers and brought back a first aid kit. "Here," she said, out of breath. "Will this help?"

"There should be a blue ice pack in there," Coach Talbot said, taking the kit.

"I'm fine," Arielle said, shakily rising to her feet. "Really."

Coach Talbot looked around at the rest of us. "Ten more laps, ladies," she said. "Get moving. McClintic, you too. We've got it under control here. And Davis, I want you to hit the showers right after we fix you up. You can come back with everyone else on Monday for tryouts. I've seen enough today."

I looked back a couple of times over my shoulder as I rounded my third lap. Arielle was heading up the hill toward the field house, holding the ice pack to her eye. Felicia and Amanda were with her.

The rest of the practice went okay, but my heart wasn't really in it. I saw Coach Talbot writing notes about everyone on her clipboard, and she nodded once or twice when I made a decent play.

But I wasn't playing as well as I could have been.

As soon as practice ended, I ran up the hill like a shot.

As I pushed open the locker-room door, I heard voices. *Good*, I thought. *They're still here.*

But then I heard Arielle say, "I can't believe she's even trying out. She's a total klutz. I mean, tripping like that? Give me a break."

I froze in the doorway. They hadn't seen me yet.

"I just hope she didn't ruin my chances of making the team. She made me look bad," Arielle went on.

"Come on, Arielle," Amanda said. "Traci didn't make you look bad. You're a great player. Everyone knows it. Of course you're going to get picked for the team."

Felicia just stood there, biting her nails again. Why didn't she say anything?

"What are you defending Traci for?" Arielle demanded. She stood up. Her eye was almost swollen shut. "You saw her. She tripped right in front of me."

"Well, Felicia and I distracted her," Amanda said. "Didn't we, Felicia?"

"Um, I guess so," Felicia mumbled.

"Ms. Southern Girl is jealous of me, that's all," Arielle said.

Okay, that was it. I couldn't stand it anymore.

"What exactly are you saying, Arielle?" I asked, stepping forward. "That I tripped you up on purpose? I'm sorry you got hurt, but you shouldn't have been so close to me in the first place."

"Come on, guys. Don't fight," Amanda pleaded. "It was just a stupid accident."

"Call it whatever you want," Arielle said. "But I've had enough. I'm going home." She picked up her fancy sports bag from the bench and pushed past me toward the door.

"Arielle, wait!" Felicia called, running after her. "I'll call you tonight, okay?" she whispered to me on her way out the door.

What? Could this actually be happening? Arielle had accused me of tripping her on purpose. And Felicia, who was supposed to be my friend, didn't even wait around to hear my side of the story?

Amanda sighed. "Just let Arielle cool off a little," she told me. "She's kind of a drama queen sometimes. But she can be nice when she wants to be."

"I honestly don't care," I fumed, heading toward my locker. I pulled off my sweatshirt. "Listen, Amanda, you don't have to wait for me. I need to take a shower and everything."

"Well, all right," Amanda said. "I'll see you tomorrow, then."

"Okay," I said, my voice muffled as I rummaged through my locker. I knew I was about to cry and I didn't want Amanda to see me.

As Amanda left, a whole bunch of girls burst into the locker room.

I decided to shower at home.

If that's what you could call 240 East Lake Road. It wasn't much more than a pile of boxes, really.

At that moment I hated my new house, my new school, and my new life.

I hated Wonder Lake.

chapter
six

Dear Diary,
  Well, today just kept getting worse and worse.
I'm not even going to write about Arielle and
soccer practice. It makes me too mad. I just had
a big talk with Mom. She says I have to join the
orchestra. I kind of liked playing clarinet in my
orchestra back in Charleston, but I can't here in
Wonder Lake! Not with Mom in charge. The
only good part is, Felicia might be in orchestra,
too. She plays the flute. Although who knows if
she still plays. She's pretty different now from
the old Felicia I knew. Anyway, she still hasn't
called me tonight like she promised. I'm sitting
right here on my bed next to the phone and it
hasn't rung once.

"Two-thirty in the music room, Traci," Mom
reminded me the next morning as I ran through the
kitchen. "Don't forget."

"How could I?" I muttered. I grabbed an apple
from the bowl on the counter. My clarinet case was
right next to it.

I was still mad at Mom about the whole orchestra thing. I almost felt like slamming the door on my way out. But I'm not that much of a brat.

I sat next to Dave on the bus. He was reading a comic book, so we didn't talk much. That was fine with me. I just stared out the window all the way to school.

As we passed a small pink building near a shopping strip, I spotted a sign in the window: PAWN SHOP. WE BUY ANYTHING!

I wondered how much I could get for my clarinet. Enough for a one-way bus fare back home to Charleston?

But something was bugging me even more than being forced to be in orchestra.

Felicia never called last night. She was probably on the phone with Arielle instead.

"Have fun at orchestra with Mom," Dave told me with a grin as we got off the bus. Then he ran over to join some guys playing Frisbee on the front lawn.

"Thanks a lot, loser!" I called after him.

It wasn't fair. How come I inherited Mom's musical genes and Dave didn't? He didn't have to take music lessons or play in the orchestra. All he did was ride his skateboard and play video games with his friends. Those were his only talents, as far as I could tell.

I saw Amanda walking into school by herself,

wearing a long Indian-print skirt. But she was way ahead of me and I couldn't catch up.

In homeroom, Amanda and Arielle weren't talking to each other.

"Hi," I said quietly to both of them as I sat down.

"Hi, Traci," Amanda said. But I couldn't tell whether she was glad to see me or not.

Arielle didn't even answer.

"Could I have a volunteer to pick up something from the office?" Mom called from the front of the room.

Amanda immediately raised her hand. "I'll go, Ms. McClintic," she said.

Arielle seemed to be very busy studying her Spanish book. Actually, I think she was hiding behind it so no one would ask her about her black eye.

It looked even worse this morning, and I felt really terrible.

But I didn't say anything to her. I just sat there and drew heart and flower doodles on my notebook.

Then I thought of Lola, the big St. Bernard puppy, and Mr. Fiol and the animal shelter. If we were all fighting, what would happen to the fund-raiser? Tomorrow, Felicia, Amanda, Arielle, and I were supposed to meet at Wonder Lake Pizza to make plans.

I wrote a little reminder note to Arielle and dropped it on the floor near her chair. But she didn't open it. She just kicked the note away.

*   *   *

57

Felicia wasn't at lunch. I thought I spotted her through the glass doors of the library, but I wasn't sure.

So what? I didn't want to speak to her, anyway.

I sat at a table in the cafeteria all by myself. I felt like the loneliest kid on the planet.

Especially when I got surrounded by a bunch of guys who kept talking about some stupid video game. They acted as if I didn't even exist.

Felicia came up to me as I was walking into math class.

"Traci, listen—" she began.

"No chitchat, girls," Mr. Reid said, before Felicia could get another word out. "We have a lot to do today."

Mr. Reid gave me the creeps. Today he was wearing a shiny purple shirt with a really ugly tie. And behind him, the blackboard was already scribbled with fractions.

Now *that* was scary.

When class was over, Mr. Reid stopped Felicia on her way out the door.

"Ms. Fiol, I wanted to talk to you about joining the math team," I heard him say.

Felicia froze and started gnawing on her thumbnail.

She gets amazing grades, although most of the time she tries to hide it. I have no idea why. I wish *I* got straight A's. Not that I'm a bad student, or anything. I do pretty well in English and Spanish. But math and science? Well, let's just say no one is asking *me* to be on the math team.

Felicia glanced at me, looking embarrassed, and followed Mr. Reid back to his desk. And maybe I'm completely paranoid, but I had a feeling she wasn't *that* embarrassed. I think she was sort of relieved not to have to talk to me.

Finally, the bell rang for Activity Period.

Time for orchestra.

When I reached the music room, the place was in total chaos.

Everyone was playing their instruments at once, seeing who could make the most noise. My mom was trying to pass out music sheets and check kids' names off the sign-up sheet.

What a mess.

I headed over to the row of cubbies along one wall where we were supposed to put our instrument cases.

I almost bumped into Felicia, who was quietly unpacking her flute.

I decided to be extra-friendly. Maybe I'd been too quick to get mad at her. My parents always say I tend to blow things out of proportion.

"Hey, Felicia," I said. "Remember when both of us wanted to be baton twirlers? We used to practice twirling sticks of driftwood at the beach."

Felicia smiled, and a familiar dimple showed up on each of her cheeks. "Do you think we'll get to wear those sparkly twirler outfits for orchestra?" she asked.

"Maybe," I said. "I could ask the orchestra leader. I know her pretty well."

We both laughed, and I glanced back at Mom. She was tapping a stick on her music stand, but no one could hear her over all the noise.

"People!" she called. "Please! We need to get started with tryouts."

Everyone ignored her.

Poor Mom. I really felt sorry for her. Even if she *was* making me do this whole orchestra thing.

I took the cubby under Felicia's and snapped open my clarinet case.

"Traci, I'm really sorry I couldn't call last night," Felicia whispered. "I had to help my dad with some new puppies. We almost lost one of them. By the time the vet came, Dad said it was too late for me to use the phone on a school night."

That made me feel a lot better. Mr. Fiol had always been pretty strict with her about rules. "That's okay," I told Felicia.

Suddenly, Mom flicked the lights in the music room on and off, and the room got completely quiet.

"All right," she said loudly. "We've wasted enough time. Anyone who does *not* want to be in orchestra please leave right now."

Does that mean me? I thought hopefully. But I didn't dare move.

The room remained silent. Way to go, Mom.

"We'll start with the string section," Mom announced. "Violins, cellos, over here, please."

"Hey, don't forget banjos!" someone called.

That could only be one person. Ryan Bradley. What was *he* doing here?

I turned around and he waggled his fingers at me.

"Aren't banjos what y'all play down south?" he asked, grinning.

I gritted my teeth.

A dark-haired boy with braces on held up his oboe. "Can I do my tryout first, Ms. McClintic?" he called. "I have to leave early. For the dentist."

"Oh dear," Mom said. "Well, okay. We'll start with woodwind instruments, then. Oboes, clarinets, up here, please."

I sighed. "Well, that's me," I told Felicia. "See ya."

"Good luck," Felicia said.

When it was my turn to play, I almost knocked over a row of music stands as I sat down.

I couldn't help it. Playing the clarinet didn't make me nervous. But having Ryan Bradley in the room did.

"Whooee, it's the music teacher's daughter," he said, in a low voice. "Guess she must be pretty good."

My face flamed. Then I tightened the reed on my clarinet so hard, it snapped in half.

Mom looked concerned. "You have another one in your case, don't you, Traci?" she asked. "We'll wait while you get it."

I hurried back to the cubbies. Felicia was already there and she handed me a new reed. But it took forever for me to replace it. My hands were shaking all over the place. Then, in the middle of my tryout piece, "Chattanooga Choo-Choo," I squeaked my clarinet so badly it sounded like a sick baby elephant.

Mom probably thought I was trying to play badly on purpose. She didn't look very pleased.

But it wasn't my fault. Honest. It was Ryan's.

String tryouts were next. I went to the back of the room again and stood next to Felicia.

"Can't wait for *this*," I told her, crossing my arms.

Ryan went last. He played a section from Beethoven's Fifth on the violin.

I couldn't believe it. He was *good*. Amazing, actually.

When Ryan finished, the room was very still for a minute. Then everyone started clapping.

"First violin for sure," Felicia whispered to me.

Ryan gave a huge, exaggerated bow. And then he played a few bars of "Dixie" really fast. Of course he had to ruin everything.

My mom looked confused. "Thank you, Ryan," she said. "I think we've heard enough from you for today."

I almost left the room right then and there. But I wanted to hear Felicia's flute tryout. She looked really nervous.

"You'll do great," I told her. "Break a leg."

Then I remembered that Amanda had said that to me just before I tripped on the track.

Felicia just nodded. I guess she didn't remember. Or maybe she was just being nice. "Thanks," she said.

Felicia played a piece of Mozart. She closed her eyes while she played, and it sounded perfect. I had a feeling Felicia, Ryan, and I were all going to be in orchestra together. I guess that was something to look forward to.

Afterward, Felicia and I walked out into the hall together.

"Is Arielle still mad at me?" I asked.

Felicia sighed. "I think so. But that cute seventh grader Scott Watson told her he'd go to her party, so she's feeling a lot better."

"The four of us are still meeting at Wonder Lake Pizza tomorrow, right?" I said. "To talk about the fund-raiser?"

"Well, I'll be there," Felicia promised, and it sounded like she was really looking forward to it. "Sorry, Traci, I've got to run and catch my bus. See you tomorrow!"

Finally, something good had happened. I wasn't completely over my lousy orchestra practice, but who cared about Ryan Bradley and his stupid jokes? At least Felicia and I were friends again.

And we had the fund-raiser to plan!

chapter
SEVEN

Scrawled on a page torn from Amanda's spiral notebook:

<u>ALL</u> <u>FOR</u> <u>PAWS</u>: IDEAS

PUBLICITY (POSTERS, FLIERS ETC.)
HAND OUT FLIERS AT MALL? BRING PETS WITH
US SO PEOPLE CAN ADOPT?
FOOD—FELICIA'S MOM'S BAKERY?
CALL MAYOR'S OFFICE/WONDER LAKE GAZETTE
BOOTH SPONSORS—PET STORE? WLMS?
WHO ELSE?
MUSIC—WWLX RADIO VAN?
"ADOPTEE OF THE MONTH"—LOLA?
WEB SITE FOR SHELTER?? GET TRACI'S
BROTHER TO HELP?
RAFFLE—PRIZE? ASK STORES TO DONATE STUFF?
WHAT ELSE??

Dave and I rode our bikes to the center of town on
Saturday. Wonder Lake isn't very big, so we got there
pretty quickly.

"This is it?" I said, looking around.

All I saw was the village green in the center, a big white church with a bell tower, the Wonder Lake Town Hall, a post office, a couple of tiny shops, a pizza place, and an ice cream store. There was a Mini-Mart, too. But that was it.

The green had a big white gazebo on it. I guess that's where most of the town's main events happened.

"Not a lot going on in good old Wonder Lake," Dave said. "Maybe I can find a skate park around here somewhere."

"Good luck," I said. "This place looks like something out of a history book. And where *is* the stupid lake, anyway? That's what I want to know."

"Well, it has to be pretty big, if they named a whole town after it," Dave said, shrugging. Then his mouth dropped open. "Hey, wait a minute! I think I see a comic store over there on the corner. See ya later, Trace-Face."

Trust my brother to sniff out the only comic store within miles.

I checked my watch. Eleven-thirty. I was supposed to meet Felicia, Amanda, and Arielle at noon.

I kind of hoped Arielle wouldn't show up. I really didn't want to see her, after all the mean things she'd said about me. Plus, seeing her black eye always made me feel ten times worse. And she hadn't seemed that into the idea of the fund-raiser in the first place.

I locked my bike and walked over to the green.

To my surprise, Felicia was sitting on one of the benches reading a teen magazine. Why hadn't I noticed her before? She was wearing a yellow flowered sundress and her hair was clipped back with tiny butterfly barrettes.

I was wearing a plain white T-shirt and cut-off jeans. Not exactly a fashion statement.

"Hi," I said, sitting down next to her.

"Oh, hi, Traci," she said. "You're early."

"You are, too," I said.

"Well, that's my parents' bakery across the way," Felicia said. "I'm staying at Mom's for the weekend, so I didn't have far to go."

"Guess you guys never go hungry," I said.

Felicia looked confused.

"I mean, since you have the bakery right there," I added.

Maybe that was a dumb thing to say. But to tell you the truth, I couldn't think of much else. For some reason, I felt a little awkward talking to Felicia now.

Weren't best friends supposed to talk about all kinds of things nonstop? Felicia sure was a lot quieter than she used to be. But maybe it was my imagination. Everything had seemed okay between us at orchestra yesterday.

"What are you reading?" I asked.

Felicia shrugged. "Oh, nothing, really." She seemed a little embarrassed. "Just a stupid article."

I glanced down at the page. "How to Be Popular"? Ugh.

Felicia flipped the magazine shut. "Actually, I was checking out the fashion stuff," she said. "I'm trying to decide what to wear to Arielle's party. If she has it, I mean," she added quickly.

I looked down at my sneakers. "I guess I won't be invited now," I said.

"Sure you will, Traci," Felicia said. She sounded hopeful. "Arielle won't stay mad at you forever."

"Well, I don't care anyway," I said, even though that wasn't true. I hopped off of the bench. "Come on, it's almost noon. Time for our meeting."

Wonder Lake Pizza wasn't very big, but it smelled amazing. The dark-haired man behind the counter gave us a huge smile when we walked in.

"Sal, this is my friend Traci," Felicia told him. "She just moved here."

"Is that so?" Sal stuck out his hand. "Welcome, Traci. So what'll it be today, girls?"

"We're meeting friends here soon," Felicia said. "We'll just have Cokes for now, thanks."

Amanda walked in just as we were sitting down. She was wearing embroidered jeans and a gauzy, lavender blouse, and carrying a purple notebook and a matching organizer book.

My dad gave my mom one of those organizer things for Christmas. She doesn't use it much. Maybe she should.

"Hi, guys," Amanda said. "Let's get started right away, okay? We have tons to do and only a week left till the big day."

Wow. *She sure gets down to business*, I told myself.

Amanda handed Felicia and me each a typed list. "I thought maybe we could start with these ideas."

I looked down at the list. I have to say, I was impressed. Amanda *was* super-organized.

"Shouldn't we wait for Arielle?" Felicia asked. "She's still coming, right, Amanda?"

"We can start without her," Amanda said. "But she's definitely coming. I talked to her last night."

"You did?" I said in surprise. How could the two of them make up so quickly? From what I'd seen in homeroom they were barely talking.

Sal came over to take our order.

"One mushroom and pepper and one broccoli," Amanda told him.

Felicia hesitated. "What do you think Arielle will want?" she asked.

Amanda waved her hand. "The broccoli's for her," she said. "Arielle's on a health kick."

"I'll have pepperoni," I told Sal.

"Broccoli for me, too," Felicia said.

Sal chuckled. "I thought you were an extra-cheese and sausage fan, Felicia," he said.

Felicia bit her lip. "Not anymore," she said.

I started to get this strange feeling in my stomach.

And it wasn't because I was hungry. Was I crazy, or was Felicia trying to copy Arielle?

"What would you think of playing games where we could pair up animals with people who might adopt them?" Amanda asked. "You know, like an obstacle course or Frisbee?"

"That's a great idea!" I said. "That way, the new owners and pets could really get to know each other."

"But the most important thing to start with is publicity," Amanda said. "Felicia, what has your dad done so far?"

"Huh?" Felicia was looking out the window. "Um, I'm not sure," she answered quickly. "But I'll ask him."

"I think we should hand out fliers at the mall," I said. "There *is* a mall around here, right?"

"Of course," Amanda said. "The Wonder Lake Shopping Center. It's a little ways out of town, actually."

"We'd have to do it tomorrow, I guess," I said. "Because it's the only weekend day we have left. Maybe I could make up some fliers on the computer tonight."

"Perfect," Amanda said, writing that down in her notebook.

Felicia kept glancing toward the door, obviously looking for Arielle.

What was the matter with her, anyway? Didn't she care about helping her own dad—and all of those poor animals?

Amanda didn't seem to notice. "One of our biggest problems is going to be food," she said. "Felicia, do you think maybe your mom could donate some snacks from the bakery?"

"What?" Felicia said, startled.

"You know, cookies or brownies or something? We could put a little sign next to them saying "Fiol's Bakery."

"Sure," Felicia said distractedly. "That'd be good publicity for my mom, too."

Sal brought our pizza slices. "Enjoy," he said.

Just then, the door swung open.

Princess Arielle had finally arrived. She looked great in a plaid halter top and black capri pants.

"Hi, everybody," she said breathlessly, sliding into a seat.

When she flipped back her hair I noticed that her eye looked a lot better. I breathed a sigh of relief. Was she still mad at me about that? I wondered.

"Oh good, Amanda, you ordered me broccoli," Arielle breezed on. "Sorry I'm so late."

"That's okay," Felicia told her.

"Well, you'll all understand when you hear why," Arielle said.

Amanda put down her slice. "Okay, why?"

Arielle paused for dramatic effect. "My parents said I couldn't have my party!"

Felicia gasped. Amanda frowned. "You're kidding," she said.

I didn't say anything. I figured maybe I should stay as quiet as possible until I knew whether or not Arielle was talking to me.

"My parents said they had to go on some stupid business trips," Arielle went on. "For two weekends in a row, can you believe it? So I have to have my party sooner than I thought."

"So when is the party now?" Felicia asked eagerly.

"Next Saturday," Arielle said. "I've already booked the DJ. Isn't that great?"

I almost choked on my pizza. That was the very same day as the All For Paws fund-raiser!

chapter
EIGHT

**Note passed from Traci to Amanda
on Wonder Lake Pizza napkin:**

*NEXT Saturday? Hello??!!
Make her change her mind!*

Felicia and Amanda and I exchanged glances.

How could Arielle have forgotten about the fundraiser?

"I've been off the phone all morning, inviting people," Arielle gushed. "Practically half the kids at school are coming—the cool ones, anyway. Even some of the seventh and eighth graders I know said they'd come."

Arielle was really on a roll now. "But that's not the best part," she said. She helped herself to a gulp of Amanda's soda. "Ready?"

The rest of us just sat there, still stunned. Felicia started to bite her pinky nail.

"The whole guys' soccer team said *yes*!" Arielle finished gleefully.

73

I slipped Amanda a note on my napkin. Arielle was so excited, she didn't even notice.

"Well, not the *whole* team," she corrected herself. "Devon Tyler's away this weekend, so I couldn't call him. But I'll find out first thing at school on Monday."

Amanda cleared her throat. "Um, Arielle?"

Arielle twirled a piece of broccoli on a plastic fork. "Yes?"

"Aren't you forgetting something?"

Felicia was starting on the rest of her nails now.

Arielle frowned. "Oh, I know it's the same day we said we'd do the fund-raiser for the animal shelter. But I can't change the party, and we haven't even started planning the fund-raiser. So let's just move the fund-raiser thing to another day."

The rest of us just stared at her blankly.

"I'm sure Felicia's dad won't mind if we have it a week later. Right, Felicia?" Arielle said.

Felicia took a deep breath. "Actually, I don't think we can move the date," she said. "My dad already got a permit to use the green and everything."

"You'll have to change your party," Amanda told Arielle.

Arielle's mouth dropped open. "You're kidding, right?"

"No," I said. "We're not. We promised we'd do this for the shelter, and a promise is a promise."

"Listen," Arielle hissed in a low whisper. "I am *not*

74

canceling my party. Not after all the trouble I went through to convince my parents to let me have it in the first place. It may not be a big deal to you guys, but it is to me."

"I'm sure everyone would understand," Amanda said.

"I just can't believe my best friends"—Arielle gave me a sideways "not you" look—"would desert me on the most important day of my life. Because of a stupid *fund-raiser?*"

"We're not deserting you, Arielle," Felicia assured her quickly.

"You can have the party another weekend," Amanda said. "Like, in October or something. It could be a Halloween party."

"October?" Arielle looked shocked. "You don't get it. I want this party to be the first one of the school year. And the best one." She sat back in her chair and crossed her arms. "You'll just have to ditch the fund-raiser."

What a spoiled brat! "No way," I said, my voice rising. "The animal shelter is a lot more important than your party. Isn't it, Felicia?"

"They're both important," Felicia said.

I looked to Amanda for help.

"Listen, Arielle," Amanda said in a soothing voice. "No one's saying that your party isn't as important as raising money for a worthy cause. It's just that—"

I couldn't stand this. "Arielle, how can you be so

selfish?" I broke in. "Those animals need our help. Mr. Fiol needs our help. And Amanda and Felicia and I have been here since noon, making plans. You didn't even bother showing up until a few minutes ago."

Arielle glared at me. "Who do you think you are?" she said. "Your opinion doesn't count. You hardly even *know* any of us."

"That's not true," I said. I turned to Felicia.

She looked away, biting her lip.

"Stop it, Arielle," Amanda jumped in. "Traci's right. You're being a total jerk about this. There are plenty of other weekends to have your party."

"Oh, really?" Arielle's green eyes narrowed. "Then fine. You and your new best friend, Ms. Southern Girl, can just consider yourself *un*-invited."

"Who'd want to go to your party anyway?" I said hotly.

This time, all of us turned to Felicia.

She stared down at the table.

"I'm with Arielle," she said quietly.

The rest of us were silent.

I couldn't believe my ears.

How could Felicia even think of deserting the fund-raiser for some dumb party?

Especially Arielle's.

"Felicia, what about all the animals?" I said.

"And your dad. Won't he be really disappointed?" Amanda asked.

Felicia didn't answer.

"Hey, it's her choice," Arielle said. "And she's making the right one. If I have my party next Saturday, it'll be the first major social event of the school year. We're not in elementary school anymore," she added. "This is *important.*"

I was so mad, I was afraid to say anything more. I threw down a bunch of crumpled dollar bills and stormed out of Wonder Lake Pizza.

I didn't care that Sal was staring at me as I pushed through the screen door. I didn't care what any of them thought.

Amanda ran after me. "Traci, wait!" she called.

I just shook my head and kept walking. I couldn't remember where I'd locked my bike.

"Traci," Amanda tried again, catching up with me. "Stop a second, please? I need to talk to you."

I stopped. After all, Amanda wasn't the one I was mad at.

It was Arielle.

No, Felicia.

Okay, both of them.

"Sorry, Amanda," I said. "Thanks for coming after me. But I've already made up my mind. I'm working on the fund-raiser, just like we planned."

"Me too," Amanda said.

"Really?" I said, surprised. Would Amanda actually stand up to Arielle like that?

Amanda sighed. "Well, it won't be easy," she said. "I have to warn you. Arielle can be pretty difficult sometimes. Going against her could be a big mistake."

"I think I've already figured that out," I sighed.

"Well, maybe I can change their minds," Amanda said. "But I doubt it. Once Arielle makes up her mind about something, that's it. She almost never changes it."

I gave Amanda a weak grin. "I guess I can be kind of stubborn, too."

Amanda grinned back. "I think I've already figured that out," she said.

"But the animals need us," I said with a shrug. "Especially Lola. What else can we do?"

"Right." Amanda nodded. "Well, I'd better get back and pay for my pizza. But listen, don't think too badly of Arielle, okay?"

I kicked at an imaginary pebble on the sidewalk.

"I've known her since before kindergarten," Amanda went on. "And she's actually a pretty nice person. I mean, she can be a little selfish sometimes. . . ."

I looked up at Amanda and raised my eyebrows.

"Okay, maybe a *lot* selfish," Amanda admitted. "But she always comes around if you give her a chance."

I was dying to tell Amanda what I really thought. That I couldn't believe she was wasting her time being friends with a snob like Arielle Davis.

But this time I stayed quiet.

"I need to get started on those fliers," I said. "I'm going to hand them out at the mall tomorrow, no matter what. I don't care if I have to do it all by myself."

"I'll be there," Amanda promised, turning to go. "Even if Arielle and Felicia won't help. We're going to save the Wonder Lake Animal Shelter. Okay?"

I forced a smile. "Okay," I said.

Amanda broke into a jog. "See you tomorrow!" she called over her shoulder.

I finally found my bike and pedaled as fast as I could toward home.

A few blocks out of town, I realized I was totally lost.

I rode back to the green and stopped at the first place on the corner. Bette's Coffee Shoppe. I sure wasn't going back into Wonder Lake Pizza.

A skinny red-haired waitress came up to me with a menu. She was wearing a pink uniform and a plastic tag that said "Darlene."

"Um, thanks, but I just need directions," I said. "To East Lake Road. That's where I live."

Darlene seemed to think that was pretty funny. She laughed, and her eyes crinkled up into her black eyeliner. "You don't know how to get to your own house, honey?"

"I just moved here," I told her.

Darlene drew me a little map on the back of a blank

order slip. "That's where you want to go," she explained.

"Thanks a lot," I said, turning away.

"Wait, sweetie," Darlene said, rushing behind the counter. "Let me cut you a slice of this nice cake to go. On the house. Since you're new to Wonder Lake and all."

I thanked her and walked back out to my bike.

I really wasn't hungry, but I knew Dave would eat the cake up in two bites.

On the way home, I passed a sign that I hadn't seen before. It was very old and the letters were hard to read. WONDER LAKE RECREATION AREA, it said, pointing down a dirt road. So *that's* where the lake was.

If I hadn't been in such a bad mood I would have turned down the road to check it out. But all I could think about right then was saving the Wonder Lake Animal Shelter. And Lola.

And how disappointed I was in my former friend, Felicia Fiol.

Instant Messages:
Chellsee3 / sockrgrl0

Chellsee3: Sorry I wasn't home when u e-mailed last nite. Went to the movies with Kaylie and Madison. How r u?

sockrgrl0: Not 2 good! That girl Arielle is driving

me crazy. Wonder Lake is the worst. I want to go home!

Chellsee3: Don't worry, things will get better. At least u have Felicia.

sockrgrl0: Yeah, I guess.

Chellsee3: We all miss you. Kaylie and Madison say hi.

sockrgrl0: I miss you guys too. I wish I was there.

chapter
NINE

FROM THE DESK OF ARIELLE DAVIS

PARTY CHECKLIST—URGENT!!!!

CDs, decorations (blue-and-white streamers with gold stars for WLMS colors?), punch bowls, food and soda (tons), makeup, cool new outfit (don't forget shoes), get haircut? Manicure? Napkins, plates, cups, plastic forks, etc., new volleyball net, talk to DJ, INVITE MORE PEOPLE!

"Traci, the answer is still no," my mother said, flipping a pancake onto Dave's plate.

"Please?" I tried again. "I promise I'll be careful."

Mom poured more pancake batter on the griddle. The bubbles in the batter rose and burst.

Sort of like my plans.

"I'm sorry," Mom said. "But you are *not* going alone to a strange mall in a strange town to hand out fliers to strangers."

"But you said Dave and I should try to feel at home here," I said.

Mom's only answer was to stir up more batter. Then she said, "Why don't you stay home and practice your clarinet? You sounded a little rusty at the orchestra tryouts."

Uh-oh. Dangerous territory. Time to change strategies. "Dad?" I said hopefully.

"Hmmm?" Dad said, looking up from his paper. He looked very tired. He'd been working really hard at the clinic, trying to set everything up. None of us had seen him much since we moved. The job at the new clinic was supposed to give him more family time, but so far it was doing just the opposite.

"I'll go with Traci," Dave offered suddenly. He was sitting at the table in his T-shirt and sweats, scarfing down a bowl of cereal.

"You will?" I said, completely shocked. Sometimes Dave is actually a pretty decent brother.

Dad stirred his coffee. "If Dave goes, it might be okay," he said. He glanced at my mom. "I have some things to pick up at Home Depot, so I could check on them while I'm there."

Mom sighed. "Fine," she said.

"Oh, thank you!" I cried. "I'll go get ready right now." I ran upstairs to get dressed and call Amanda and Mr. Fiol to make last-minute arrangements.

*   *   *

We rode our bikes all the way to the mall. It's on the outskirts of town, so it was a long ride. We didn't get there until one.

"Where do you want to set up the card table?" Dave asked.

I looked around and saw a store called Purr-fect Pets near the main entrance. It *was* perfect.

"Over there," I said, pointing.

We had to ask the pet store owner's permission, but luckily she said yes right away. "For the Wonder Lake Animal Shelter?" she said. "Absolutely! It might help bring people to my store, too."

I carefully spread out the fliers on the table. Dave taped the big All For Paws sign I'd made to the front of it.

"We'll have to talk to as many people as we can," I said. "And we can't hand out all the fliers too early."

"I'll do the fliers," Dave said. "You can do the talking." He grinned. "Since you're such a motormouth."

"Ha ha," I said sarcastically. Even when he was being nice, my brother had to be a pain.

People started stopping by the table right away, although I think some of them were just looking for free stuff. At first we were so busy that I almost forgot about Amanda. I checked my watch. Where was she? It was almost a quarter to two.

Had she changed her mind?

Mr. Fiol arrived about half an hour later. He brought a whole bunch of animals with him. Even Lola!

"I called some extra volunteers to help at the shelter," he explained. "Weekends are our busiest times, so I wasn't sure I could get away, otherwise."

"I'm so glad you brought some of the animals," I said. I gave Lola a big hug.

Dave reached down to pat her and Lola jumped up and licked his face. Dave laughed and scratched her ears. His face was already getting blotchy and his eyes were watering, but he didn't seem to mind.

Mr. Fiol smiled. "I thought if people saw these guys, they wouldn't be able to resist them," he said.

One of the cats was scratching at its carrier and yowling loudly.

"Cut it out, Mr. Kitty," I told him. "Don't you want to make a good first impression?"

Dave peered into the carrier. Then he began to sneeze. "Excuse me," he said quickly. "I'm going to buy a box of tissues. I'll be right back." He bounded across the mall to the drugstore.

"Traci, I have some good news," Mr. Fiol told me as we both tried to calm down a whimpering poodle puppy. "Thanks to those phone calls Amanda made yesterday afternoon, WWLX and WLFM-TV both said they'd give the fund-raiser coverage as a public service."

"That's great!" I said. "Hey, maybe Lola will become one of those dog TV stars."

Next to me, Lola thumped her tail.

A woman came up to peer into a cage of adorable kittens.

"Aren't they sweet," she said.

"They sure are. And they need homes," I told her, taking two of the kittens out of the cage.

The woman looked doubtful. "Have they had all of their shots?" she asked.

Mr. Fiol nodded. "The vet says they're in perfect health," he said. "But they'll need to be spayed in about two months."

"Can I hold them?" the woman asked. "I might be able to take just one, but . . ."

"We're trying to get them adopted in pairs," I said quickly. "That way, they'll always have company."

"Oh. Well, I guess that makes sense," the woman said, smiling.

She ended up adopting the little red kitten *and* her black-and-white sister!

Everything was going just the way we'd planned. Well, except for the fact that Amanda wasn't there.

At least I had Dave. He was really trying to help, even though he kept sneezing all over the place and running to the rest room to wash his hands.

Suddenly, I saw Amanda, running through the mall entrance, looking frantic. "I'm so sorry!" she told us breathlessly when she reached our table. "I had to baby-sit my little brothers and sister until my stepmom got home."

"That's okay," I said. "We're just glad you came."

"So far, your mall idea has been a big success," Mr. Fiol said. "Some of the animals have already been adopted."

"That's great," Amanda cried.

"But not Lola," I said. I looked down sadly at the St. Bernard puppy. She kept tugging on her leash, trying to follow any shoppers who walked by.

Amanda went right to work, handing out fliers. "I think we're going to run out of those soon," I told her.

"Really?" Amanda said, frowning. "Okay, I'll run down to the copy shop and make some more."

"I'll go with you," I offered.

Amanda shook her head. "No, you stay here and keep talking to people," she said. "There's no sense in us both going."

That made sense, I guess. But to tell you the truth, I wouldn't have minded taking a little break and catching up with Amanda. "Hey, would you get me a soda?" I asked.

"Sure, if I get a chance," Amanda said, turning to go.

"Okay, never mind," I said. I mean, if it was that big a deal to her I could get my own soda.

Amanda stopped when she heard the hurt tone in

my voice. "Sorry, Traci," she said. "It's just that we have a job to do. . . ." Her voice trailed away.

"No problem," I said quickly. "I'll get something later. Don't worry about it."

Amanda was right, we did have a job to do. But I still couldn't help feeling a little stung.

When Amanda came back with more fliers, we both worked at the table for a while. Neither of us mentioned Arielle or Felicia. In fact, we didn't talk about anything but the job at hand.

"Hey, Felicia and I had orchestra chair tryouts yesterday," I said, trying to start a normal conversation. "Everyone is going to make it, though."

Amanda nodded, but she didn't seem to be listening. She was looking across the mall. "There's a whole group of kids headed this way," she said. "Maybe we should bring out some of the kittens and put them on the table."

Amanda was completely focused on giving away fliers and getting animals adopted and telling people about the fund-raiser. I couldn't help wondering: Were Amanda and I really friends? Or was she just hanging out with me because we were both working for a good cause?

"Don't look now," I told Amanda in a low voice. "But Felicia and Arielle are heading this way."

"Really?" Amanda gazed down the mall distractedly. "I was wondering when they'd show up."

"I don't think they're here to help us," I said.

Arielle and Felicia were just coming out of About Face, a trendy makeup store. They both had their hands full of shopping bags.

"Do you think they'll come over here?" I whispered to Amanda. Mr. Fiol was standing near us, talking to a young couple who were thinking of adopting a rabbit.

"No," Amanda said. "Probably not."

"Do you think one of us should go over and talk to them?" I asked, frowning.

Amanda bent down and adjusted the water bottle on the side of the rabbit's cage. "No," she said. "They know we're here. If they want to talk to us, they can come over and talk to us." There was an edge to her voice that hadn't been there before. I could tell she was upset.

I glanced over at Mr. Fiol. I could see that he was watching Felicia and Arielle, just like we were. And he didn't look happy either.

Amanda suddenly grabbed a bunch of fliers from the table. Then she headed toward a group of older women who were resting on a bench. "Pets are great company," I heard her say. "And cats are especially easy to take care of."

Amanda was amazing. Even seeing her best friend shopping for a party that she wasn't invited to couldn't stop her.

I kept looking back at Felicia and Arielle. The two of them had stopped at a snack stand. I noticed that Felicia was wearing black capri pants, just like Arielle had worn yesterday. She was so obviously copying Arielle. It was kind of sad.

To my surprise, Felicia glanced over at the All For Paws table and waved. I waved back, but then I realized she wasn't waving at me. She was waving at her dad.

Maybe it was my imagination. But I thought Felicia looked kind of guilty. And maybe a little sad.

But then Arielle handed her a big ice cream cone with chocolate sprinkles on it. That cheered Felicia up, I could tell. So did the two cute boys who stopped by the snack stand to talk to her and Arielle.

Arielle still had a black eye. But she still looked really pretty. And totally sure of herself.

I was so busy watching them that I didn't realize Mr. Fiol was standing beside me.

"I guess Felicia is playing hooky today," he said, smiling wistfully. "She said Arielle needed her help getting ready for a party."

I wasn't sure what to say. Was Mr. Fiol disappointed that Felicia wasn't helping us? Did he know that the party was on the same day as the fund-raiser?

"Sometimes I think Felicia doesn't enjoy working at the shelter," he went on. He sighed. "But she does spend a lot of time there. She needs a break sometimes."

"Excuse me? Mr. Fiol?" A sandy-haired man in a tweed jacket was standing in front of the table.

"Yes?" Mr. Fiol said.

"I'm Bob Kassin, with the *Wonder Lake Gazette*," the man said. "Could I please have a few minutes of your time?"

Mr. Fiol and the reporter left to find a quiet spot to talk. I watched as Felicia and Arielle headed into the trendy clothing store across the way.

"They sure are doing a lot of shopping," I told Amanda when she came back to the table.

Amanda shrugged. "Yeah, well, Arielle's getting everything for her party. She's probably buying up half the mall."

Amanda was acting as if she didn't care. But I wasn't sure if I believed it.

"Hi, Traci," a boy's voice said behind me.

I almost fell over when I looked up and saw who it was. Ryan Bradley!

"What are you doing here?" I said.

"I'm with my dad," Ryan answered. "We're checking out the sports store for Patrick's birthday. I saw you and Amanda over here and . . ." He shrugged.

"Oh," I said. I couldn't think of anything else to say. Why did this guy always make me feel so stupid?

"Do you, um, have any pets at home?" I asked.

"No," Ryan said. "Do you?"

"I wish I could," I told him with a sigh. "But my brother has really bad allergies." I pointed to Dave, who was trying to calm down a nervous German shepherd. His eyes were all puffy and swollen, like he'd been crying.

"That's too bad," Ryan said.

Just then, Amanda walked up to us, leading Lola. "Hi, Ryan," she said. Then she turned to me. "No luck so far finding any takers for Lola. I think everyone is afraid she's going to get too big."

"Or maybe it's all that drooling," Ryan said.

Lola was sitting at his feet, looking up at him adoringly. Her tongue was hanging out and there was already a pool of drool on the mall floor.

"Hey, doggie," he said, giving her a friendly pat.

"That's Lola," I said. "She's my favorite. I wish I could adopt her myself. And if we don't find her a home soon, I don't know what'll happen to her."

"I'm sure you'll find someone," Ryan said. He frowned. "Do you think maybe you should give her some water or something? She looks kind of thirsty."

"I'll go," Amanda said quickly. She handed me Lola's leash. "I'll get some paper towels from the pet store, too, to clean up all this drool."

"So are you coming to the All For Paws fundraiser on Saturday?" I asked Ryan. For some reason, he wasn't making me feel so nervous anymore. But it was time to get back to business.

Ryan looked over his shoulder. Arielle and Felicia were standing by the escalators now, talking and laughing with a whole bunch of WLMS kids. The two of them were carrying even more bags now.

"Uh, I'm not sure what I'm doing Saturday," he said.

"Oh," I said, disappointed. Duh. Of course Ryan would be going to Arielle's party. He didn't care about helping the animal shelter. He wanted to hang out with all the other popular kids.

"Well, I'd better head off," Ryan said. He gave Lola one more pat. "I think I see my dad over there."

"Sure," I said. Lola and I watched Ryan go. Lola seemed really disappointed, too.

"Ryan really likes you," Amanda said, as she came up with two rolls of paper towels and a fresh dish of water. "I can tell."

"What?" I said, startled.

"It's so obvious," Amanda said. "The way he's always teasing you and trying to hang around you."

"I don't think so," I said. "Ryan was paying attention to Lola, not me."

"Right," Amanda said.

Dave came up to us then, holding a kitten out in front of him. "Uh, can you take this one for a minute?" he said. "I'm really dying here."

"No problem," Amanda said quickly, reaching for the kitten. "Maybe you should take a break."

Dave wiped his eyes with his sleeve. "Yeah, I think you're right. I'll be back in a sec, okay?"

"I can't believe *that's* the dork brother you're always complaining about," Amanda whispered as soon as Dave was out of earshot.

"Well," I answered, "he's actually being pretty nice today."

"I think he's kind of cute," Amanda said, watching Dave lope to the nearest men's room.

Dave? Cute?

I thought Amanda needed to get her eyes checked. But as brothers went, I guess Dave was okay. If you liked freckled skateboard geeks.

At least Amanda and I were getting to know each other better.

Suddenly, I heard laughing.

A whole crowd of WLMS students was headed toward our table.

Great, I thought. Here's our big chance to tell them about All For Paws.

I scooped up a whole bunch of fliers and headed toward the group.

"Traci, wait!" Amanda said.

It was a good thing she stopped me before it was too late.

In the middle of the crowd was Princess Arielle.

"So you can all e-mail me your song requests for the party," I heard her saying. "And I'll give them to the DJ."

Felicia was walking beside Arielle, carrying half of Arielle's bags. And she didn't look sad anymore. She was practically glowing.

I quickly stepped back.

Arielle and Felicia and all of the other kids walked right past us. They headed straight toward the sliding glass doors, without a glance at our table or any of the animals.

Luckily, Mr. Fiol had his back turned, so he didn't notice.

Amanda frowned. "I hope some of those kids will come to the fund-raiser," she said. "But somehow I doubt it."

"They'll all be going to Arielle's party," I said, throwing the fliers back on the table. "Along with the rest of the world."

"We'll just have to try harder, then," Amanda said. She sounded determined. "We'll really have to talk up All For Paws at school this week."

"I hear you," I said, sighing. Lola looked up at me with pleading brown eyes. "Don't worry," I told her. "Everything's going to be okay."

For the rest of the afternoon, we tried to get people to pay attention to All For Paws.

But inside, I knew who would be getting all the attention.

Arielle.

"And Felicia, my ex-best friend, will be running along behind her," I muttered. "Like a little puppy."

Lola wagged her tail. "Oops, sorry," I told her. "I didn't mean it that way."

But I knew it was true.

chapter
TEN

Message left on the McClintics' answering machine:

Hey, Traci, it's Amanda. Guess what? I've gotten tons of calls and e-mails about All For Paws! People really want to help! Maybe everything's going to be okay after all. Oh, and can you bring more poster board and markers to school tomorrow? We're going to need them. Bye!

"Hey, Traci, hand me that tape, will you?" Amanda asked.

The two of us were putting up posters on the wall outside the science lab. Amanda was balanced on a small step stool.

"I think the paint may still be wet," I warned.

"I know. I just finished them this morning," Amanda said with a sigh. "I had the worst time getting them to school." She turned and held up her hands to show me the streaks of blue paint on her palms.

"Good luck at soccer today, Arielle," I heard a voice call.

I turned to see Arielle walking down the hall with Felicia, heading toward their fifth-period Spanish class. They'd walked right by us without stopping to say hello.

Soccer. I froze right in the middle of tearing off another piece of tape. I'd forgotten all about the try-outs. First cuts were today after school.

"What's the matter, Traci?" Amanda asked. She climbed down from the step stool. "Just give me that whole roll, okay?"

I handed her the tape. "Sorry," I said.

Amanda frowned at me. "You *are* going to soccer tryouts, aren't you?" she said.

I looked down at the floor. "No, I guess not," I said. "I forgot all about it."

"How could you forget?" Amanda scolded. "Do you have your soccer stuff with you?"

"Well, yeah," I said. "It's still in my locker. But we're going to put up more posters in town after school, remember?"

"Don't worry about that," Amanda said. "I've got it covered."

"Really?" I said. "Gee, thanks." I took another piece of tape from the pocket of my jeans. "But I was kind of thinking maybe I shouldn't go out for the Muskrats anyway. My mom wants me to do orchestra, and Arielle—"

"Hey, forget about Arielle," Amanda said. "She's

just trying to bug you. You're a good player, Traci. I think Arielle's actually worried you may get her position. You can't just give up."

"I can't?" I said doubtfully.

Amanda shook her head firmly. "Besides, Arielle *wants* you to try out. She knows you're good, and she wants to prove that she's better than you."

I frowned. "She's not better, she's just a lot more competitive," I scoffed. "But okay, I'll go to the try-outs. Promise you'll call me tonight and tell me how everything went in town, though, okay?"

Amanda grinned. "Don't worry. I'll make sure every store has an All For Paws sign in the window. I promise."

After school, as I was getting my sports bag out of my locker, Ryan Bradley came over to talk to me.

"Hi, Dixie Chick," he said. "Looks like you got all your posters up for the fund-raiser."

I just nodded, remembering what Amanda had said about Ryan liking me. He'd called me Dixie Chick again, but I decided to ignore it. Maybe he meant the nickname in a nice way. He had seemed so friendly at the mall yesterday.

Could Amanda be right? Did Ryan actually *like* me?

I closed the door of my locker and twisted the lock. "We still have a lot more to do," I said.

Ryan pointed to my bag. "You're trying out for

soccer, right? My brother plays on the varsity guys' team."

"Yeah, I'm going to tryouts now," I said. "I'm not sure I'll make it through first cuts, though. Arielle and I play the same position."

He nodded. "Center forward, right? Well, good luck."

"Thanks," I said. I slung my bag over my shoulder and started to walk away.

"Hey, Traci!" Ryan called after me. "You're still going to be in orchestra, right?"

I didn't know how to answer. My mom and I hadn't exactly worked that out yet.

"Maybe," I called back.

Then I headed down to the locker room. *Here goes nothing*, I thought.

I took a deep breath and pushed open the locker room door.

There was a lot more tension in the air this time. I could definitely feel it. The locker room was totally silent.

None of the girls even looked up as I walked in. But I was careful to choose a locker on the other side of the room from Arielle's.

Arielle was already there, in a white T-shirt and blue soccer shorts. She was stretching out on the floor.

She didn't look at me or anyone else. She was totally concentrating on the tryouts, I could tell. It was kind of intimidating to see how focused she was.

Coach Talbot walked into the locker room, all business with her clipboard. "First we'll go through a few drills," she told us, when we were all out on the field. "Then we'll try a scrimmage. Assistant Coach Ferris"— she nodded to the young woman standing next to her— "will give out yellow jerseys to half of you."

I got a yellow jersey. So did Arielle. It totally ruined her big blue-and-white fashion statement.

"Davis, McClintic, I'm trying you both for center forward," Coach Talbot said. "Good luck."

I gulped. Did she have to actually *tell* us that?

I didn't look at Arielle.

She didn't look at me, either.

Focus, I told myself.

Coach Talbot blew her whistle and we all took our places on the field. I was starting off as right wing. Arielle would play center.

"I'll switch you in the next quarter," Coach told us.

As the scrimmage began, I concentrated on the game and forgot all about Arielle.

Well, almost.

She was all over the field, scoring goals right and left.

"Get out of my way, Traci," she growled, as we chased the ball down the outside line toward the goal.

I gritted my teeth. "Get out of *my* way," I told her, catching up to the ball and scoring the goal.

"Hey, Traci, where did you say you were from again?" one of the older girls asked me at the half.

"South Carolina," I answered.

Another girl grinned. "Well, you're not too bad," she said. "For a rookie."

I could tell Arielle didn't like that much. Her face was flushed, but she wasn't hot. She was mad.

Or maybe she was just worried. I couldn't tell.

The second half went the same as the first, except I played center and Arielle played right wing.

From the corner of my eye, I saw Coach Talbot check her watch. "Two minutes!" she called.

Someone passed me the ball. I moved toward the opposing goal, dodging defenders. I was almost in scoring position.

I could make it.

But another defender was coming up on my left. I hesitated. Should I take the shot?

Or pass it to Arielle?

She was in a better position, right in front of the goal, completely open.

But I really wanted to score that goal.

I made my decision.

I passed the ball to Arielle, and she put it past the goalie easily.

Coach Talbot gave a sharp blast on her whistle. Tryouts were over for the day.

Some of the girls ran up to me and we slapped palms.

"Good going, Traci," one of them said. "Nice assist."

No one said anything to Arielle. That's because she'd already walked off the field.

When I went back to the sidelines for my water bottle, Coach Talbot came up to me. "Excellent teamwork, McClintic," she said. "You made the right call out there. Quick thinking. That's what we're looking for."

"Thanks," I said. I'd made the right decision after all!

Back in the locker room, all of the girls were chattering excitedly. The cut list was going to be posted outside in fifteen minutes.

I took an extra-long shower, letting the hot water run over my sore muscles.

It sounded as if I'd made the cut. This time, anyway. But what about Arielle?

I was the last one out of the locker room. All the other girls were gathered around a list posted on the bulletin board.

"I made it!" one girl squealed.

"Me too!" another girl said, hugging her.

Other girls weren't so lucky. I saw one of them wipe tears from her eyes and run back into the locker room.

A few girls were grumbling. "Coach Talbot's a jerk, anyway," I heard one of them say.

I waited for most of the crowd to leave before I checked the list.

There it was. McClintic. I'd made first cuts!

I looked back at the list. I couldn't help myself. There it was, near the top. Davis. Arielle had made first cuts, too.

The locker room door opened and Arielle came out. Her face was flushed and she had a streak of dirt on one cheek. A piece of hair had escaped from her ponytail.

"Congratulations," I said, trying a smile.

Arielle didn't return my smile.

"I already talked to Coach Talbot," she said, tucking her hair behind her ear. "We're both still up for center forward." Her voice sounded so threatening it sounded like she was saying, "Next time, I'm bringing you down."

I gulped. "That's great," I said weakly.

Arielle nodded. "See you at second cuts on Wednesday," she said, turning abruptly away.

I stared after her.

I had no idea which one of us would make center forward in the end.

But one thing was definitely clear.

Arielle hated my guts.

chapter
ELEVEN

E-mail from Chellsee3 to sockrgrl0:

Hey, WHERE R U?????!!! Hope things are going lots better. How were tryouts? Did u make it thru first cuts? I hope so. Our first Panthers game is in 2 weeks. Don't let that Arielle girl get u down. Hi 2 Felicia. Does she remember me? XXOO

I told Mom and Dave my big soccer news at dinner that night. Dad was still at the clinic.

"So does that mean you'll make the team for sure?" Dave asked. His mouth was full of spaghetti. Gross. How could Amanda possibly think he was cute?

"Well, no," I admitted. "Not officially. But it's looking a little more hopeful now."

"That's fantastic," Mom said. She passed me the basket of garlic bread. "But do you think you'll have time to do soccer *and* orchestra?"

I took a deep breath. "Mom, I keep telling you. I

really don't want to play the clarinet anymore. Not at school, anyway."

Mom frowned. "But honey, you loved playing in your old orchestra," she said. "And you're so talented. I hate to see you give it up."

I played with my salad, pushing the croutons around on my plate.

"Does this by any chance have anything to do with the fact that I'm the music teacher at your school?" Mom asked.

Dave pointed at me with his fork and cocked his head to one side. "That *might* have something to do with it," he said. Jerk.

Mom shot him a warning glance. "David, this doesn't concern you." She turned back to me. "Is that the problem, Traci?"

I gulped. "Well, no, not exactly . . . ," I began. A little white lie was better than hurting Mom's feelings, right?

Mom sighed and got up from the table. "I guess I understand," she said, taking her dishes to the sink. She turned on the water. "I embarrass you, don't I?"

"No!" I said quickly. "That's not it at all. I'm just way too busy. I mean, if I play soccer and do orchestra and help Mr. Fiol at the animal shelter, I won't even have any time left to do homework."

The homework excuse always works. But this time, Mom seemed a little distracted.

"Maybe I shouldn't be teaching at Wonder Lake Middle School," Mom said. "It seemed like a good idea at the time. But I could just give private music lessons again, like I did back in Charleston."

Talk about feeling guilty! "Don't quit, Mom," I said. "Really."

Mom sighed and smiled tiredly at me. "It's tough being new at school, isn't it? For both of us."

I jumped up and gave her a big hug. "Hey, positive attitude," I whispered into her ear. "Remember?"

This time Mom's smile didn't look so tired. "You're right. Hey, why don't you see how the rest of your soccer tryouts go, and get the fund-raiser out of the way, and then we'll talk about orchestra again."

"Okay," I agreed. "That sounds fair."

"Hey, I'm still starving. Can I have some more spaghetti?" Dave said loudly. So much for the big mother-daughter bonding moment.

"You know where the stove is," Mom said.

"Get it yourself," I told him at the same time, and Mom and I burst out laughing.

As soon as Dave and I had finished the dishes, I ran upstairs to my room to make some more All For Paws fliers on the computer to hand out at school tomorrow.

"Traci!" Mom called from the bottom of the stairs. "Is your homework done?"

Busted! "Um, almost," I called back.

"Didn't you say you had some kind of test tomorrow?" Mom asked. She never forgets that kind of stuff.

"Yeah. Social studies," I admitted.

"No computer until you've finished studying," Mom said. Then she went back into the living room.

I sighed. I really didn't feel like studying at all. I got my social studies notebook and climbed onto my bed. But I just couldn't concentrate. Back home in Charleston I would have called one of my friends, but I didn't feel like there was anyone in Wonder Lake I could call to blab about nothing. So I just spaced out, staring at the blank white walls of my new room.

My room in our new house was bigger than my bedroom back in Charleston, but it wasn't as cozy. Our parents wouldn't let Dave and me put anything up on the walls because we were renting, they said. And my window didn't look out on the ocean anymore. All I could see was a whole bunch of pine trees.

I still hadn't seen the lake.

Finally, I opened my notebook. But instead of reading the notes I'd taken in class on the main exports of Japan, I drew little sketches of Lola. Lola with a bone in her mouth, Lola curled up on a dog bed. Lola wearing a fancy collar with rhinestones. *What would it be like to be Lola's owner?* I wondered. I could train her and take her for walks and throw her sticks and tennis balls and . . .

I was so busy daydreaming I didn't hear the phone ring.

"Traci!" Dave yelled up the stairs. "Phone!"

It was Amanda.

"Hey, Traci," she said. "How's it going?"

"Okay," I said. "I'm supposed to be studying, but . . ."

"I won't stay on long, then," Amanda said. I could hear music playing in the background. "I just wanted to congratulate you on making first cuts at soccer today."

"Thanks," I said. "I guess I lucked out."

"It wasn't luck," Amanda said. "I told you you could do it."

"How did everything go in town?" I asked. "Did you get all the fund-raiser posters put up?"

"Almost all of them," Amanda replied. "Everyone I asked was pretty nice about it. Sal took two. One for the window and one for inside."

"That's great," I told her.

Then I heard a familiar voice in the background.

"Is Arielle there with you?" I asked.

"Yeah," Amanda answered. "She came over for dinner and we're watching MTV."

"Oh," I said.

So the two of them were best friends again. Fine. They could go for days without speaking to each other, and then all of a sudden everything was hunky-dory again? Great.

"We made up this afternoon," Amanda said. "I called Arielle up when I heard she made first cuts."

I heard Arielle's voice again, but I couldn't make out what she was saying. Probably something mean about me.

Then I heard a giggle.

"Guess who else is here?" Amanda said. "Felicia. She was over at Arielle's, so she came to my house, too."

Hello? Thanks for inviting *me*.

"Well, I'd better get back to my homework," I said quickly. I wanted to get off the phone before Amanda noticed how upset I was.

"Oh, right," Amanda said. "Well, see you at school tomorrow." The music in the background was blaring even louder now. Arielle had probably turned the volume up.

"Yeah," I said. "See ya."

I hung up and stared at my stupid white walls again.

I guess the major fight I'd thought we'd been having was no big deal to any of them.

But where did that leave me?

I could understand about Amanda and Arielle. They'd been close for so long, they probably fought and made up all the time. Amanda didn't need me—she had Arielle.

But what about Felicia? Was she completely over me?

Now it was clear: I had no friends in Wonder Lake at all.

I picked up my fifth-grade yearbook from my nightstand and flipped through it.

There was Madison's picture. And Kaylie's and Kim's and Ashley's. Underneath her photo, Chelsea had written: *To Traci—Best friends 4-ever!*

Then the picture got all blurry as hot tears began to spill down my cheeks.

I couldn't stand it anymore. I grabbed the phone and punched in Chelsea's number. I just *had* to talk to her. I didn't care how late it was or how much trouble I got into.

"Hello?" Chelsea's mom answered.

"Hi, Mrs. Beaufort," I said. "It's me, Traci. Is Chelsea there?"

"I'm sorry, Traci," Chelsea's mom said. "She's down at the pier with some of the girls. But I'll tell her you called."

"Thanks," I said. I clicked off and threw my phone across my ugly bedroom.

Even my friends in Charleston had forgotten me. Madison was probably Chelsea's new best friend now.

Maybe it was a good thing I had so many activities this year. And I'd have lots of time to practice my clarinet.

Because I sure wasn't going to have a social life.

Positive attitude? Forget it.

chapter
TWELVE

Dear Diary,

Help! I don't know what to do. I promised Mr. Fiol I'd help out at the animal shelter today. But how can I go if Felicia and I aren't even speaking to each other? It would be really weird. I definitely want to see Lola, though, and Mr. Fiol needs my help. So should I go or not?

"Ms. McClintic? Are you with us?" Mr. Reid asked.

I looked up. Everyone in math was staring at me, including Felicia.

"Sorry," I said, blushing hotly. "Could you repeat the question?"

As Mr. Reid turned to scribble more fractions on the board, I slid my journal back under my math book and tried to pay attention.

But it was impossible. I still didn't know what to do about going to the shelter after school. I stole a glance at Felicia, but she was busy scribbling notes.

Oh, what should I do? I wondered.

*   *   *

I took so long deciding, I almost missed the bus. I jumped on just as the doors were closing. I could see Felicia sitting in the back. Then the bus lurched forward, and I sat down right in front, before the driver could yell at me to take a seat.

The ride to the shelter seemed a lot longer this time. I had no idea what to say to Felicia when we got there. What if she refused to talk to me?

The bus stopped and I jumped off. I hesitated for a minute in the Fiols' driveway. *Think positive*, I told myself.

Felicia stepped off the bus.

"Hi," I said. I don't think I've ever felt that awkward.

"Um, hi," Felicia said, nervously pulling on the straps on her backpack.

"I'm here to help with the animals," I told her, feeling completely stupid. But what else could I say?

"Well, come on," Felicia said, turning to walk up the driveway. "Dad's waiting for us."

Silently, I followed Felicia into a tiny office at the front of the house. Through the wall, I could hear dogs barking, cats meowing, and geese honking.

"So what should I do first?" I asked, glancing around. The room was kind of small, with only two chairs and a desk that was littered with papers.

"I'm not sure," Felicia said stiffly. "I'll go get my dad."

"Okay," I said. I sat down on a plastic chair while Felicia went to look for her father.

"Traci!" Mr. Fiol said when he came in. He smiled. "I'm so glad you're here."

"Me too," I said. It was such a relief to see him.

Felicia didn't say anything. She just went over to the desk and started filing.

Mr. Fiol clapped his hands together. "Well, the first thing we need to do is get all these hungry critters fed," he said. "Why don't we head out to the shed and I'll show you what to do?"

I followed Mr. Fiol outside. It was cloudy, so the shelter looked sort of gloomy. And the animals were even noisier than the last time I'd been there. I guess they were really hungry.

Lola was curled up in the doghouse of her fenced-in pen. She looked a little depressed.

"Hey, girl," I called. "What's the matter? Are you lonesome?"

Lola came over and licked my hand through the fence.

"I don't have anyone to play with, either," I whispered. "But that's okay. We have each other, right?"

Mr. Fiol showed me who ate what food and how much food to give each animal. Then he showed me how to use the water pump.

"There sure is a lot for me to learn," I said.

Mr. Fiol chuckled. "It gets easier," he said.

I looked down at the bags of food. "Is there enough for all of them until the fund-raiser this weekend?" I asked.

"I think so," Mr. Fiol said, his voice serious. "But we're cutting it close. Very close."

Just then, Felicia came out of the office. "Phone for you again, Dad," she called. "Something about the fund-raiser, I think."

"Okay, honey," Mr. Fiol called back. "I'll be right there."

"It's okay," I told him. "I've got everything under control here."

I hope, I added to myself. What did the ferrets eat again? And which dog needed the diet food? I couldn't remember. Probably the bulldog. He looked pretty fat.

It took me a while to get everything done. The kitten and puppy food had to be mixed with water from the pump. Then I had to stir it with a stick. It smelled pretty gross.

The animals started gobbling the food down before I could even set the bowls down.

"No wonder the shelter is running out of food so fast," I told the whole barking, meowing group. I had no idea what kind of sounds rabbits and ferrets made, but I was pretty sure they were adding to the racket somehow. "You guys are just like my brother, Dave."

Felicia came out again a few minutes later. This time, she was lugging a huge bag of chicken feed.

I ran over to pick up one end. "Wow, this is really heavy," I said.

"Do you need any help feeding?" Felicia asked.

I looked around at all the munching, slurping animals. "I think I'm okay for now," I said. But I didn't want her to go. "What else do volunteers do?" I asked.

Felicia wrinkled her nose. "Clean out the pens," she said.

"Eww. I definitely need help, then."

Felicia laughed.

And I laughed, too.

I guess that kind of broke the ice.

Together we started pulling shovels and brooms out of the supply shed. Felicia showed me how to scoop up the poop and toss it into a wheelbarrow. She wasn't at all squeamish about it, not like she'd been when Arielle was there.

"So I guess all of us have made up now," I said. "Except for me and Arielle."

I probably shouldn't have brought the subject up. But I was tired of not talking about it.

"I know," Felicia said. She frowned. "I really want us all to be friends. I mean, all four of us."

Me, friends with Arielle? I wasn't so sure about that.

I started to sweep up chicken feed from one of the pens. "Who would ever adopt a chicken?" I wondered out loud.

Felicia giggled. "Someone who likes eggs for breakfast every morning?" she said. "Really *fresh* eggs?"

I giggled, too. We were both starting to relax a little.

"So how come Arielle is so popular?" I asked. "She seems to know everyone in town."

Felicia shrugged. "I guess she does. But Wonder Lake is a small town. And Arielle's pretty outgoing."

"That's for sure," I muttered, under my breath.

Felicia frowned but she didn't say anything.

"I just don't think she's that great," I said. I tore up some newspaper to fit into the tray below the chicken coop.

"She's nice when you get to know her," Felicia said quietly. "I wish I could be more like her."

What? I almost fell into the chicken coop.

Felicia sighed. "Look, Traci. Things have changed a lot for me in the last couple of years. When my parents got divorced I kind of backed off from people. I spent a lot of time on my own. And now that I've started middle school, I want to be more, you know—more popular."

I just stared at her. I didn't know what to say. I liked Felicia just the way she was.

"I'm kind of shy, I guess," Felicia said. "Hanging out with Arielle makes me feel braver sometimes."

"Oh," I said. I wanted to understand, I really did. But I couldn't.

I definitely needed to change the subject now. "So what's the deal with Saturday? Is Arielle going to postpone her party?"

"No," Felicia answered firmly. "It's still on. But I asked my mom to donate stuff from the bakery for the fund-raiser and she said yes."

"Great," I said, halfheartedly. It was good news, but I didn't feel that happy about it. I needed to get something off my chest.

"You know, I think it really stinks that you're going to Arielle's party instead of All For Paws," I said. "I mean, what about your dad? What does he think about that?"

Felicia looked down at a patch of weeds in the grass. "Well, he's not too happy about it," she said. "But he said it was okay. My whole life can't revolve around the shelter."

For about the zillionth time since I moved to Wonder Lake, I had no idea what to say.

Luckily, Mom drove up the driveway just then. It was time to go home.

"See you tomorrow," I mumbled and hurried over to the car. I didn't even look back at Lola.

As we started to pull away, Mr. Fiol came running out of the house.

"Thanks, Traci!" he called. "See you and Amanda on Saturday!"

Felicia stood by the house, watching silently. I could feel her eyes on me all the way down the driveway.

chapter
THIRTEEN

WONDER LAKE
MIDDLE SCHOOL NEWS
GIRLS PRE-SEASON SOCCER

For anyone who doesn't have a clue, final tryouts
for Muskrat Girls' Varsity Soccer are this
Wednesday afternoon! Coach Talbot has some
tough decisions to make, with only three varsity spots
to be filled. The center forward position is being
hotly contested by two sixth graders, former
Wonder Lake Academy Lightnings star Arielle
Davis and WLMS newcomer Traci McClintic. (For
you other clueless folks, Traci's mom teaches music
here at WLMS.) Other positions up for grabs are
right wing, vacated by recently graduated Muskrats
legend Brooke Perkins, and relief goaltender. Good
luck   to   all.
Go-o-o-o State Champ Muskrats!!!!

"Ms. McClintic?" Mr. Reid called.

I was so busy worrying about soccer tryouts, I

thought he was talking to my mother.

"Traci?" Mr. Reid said again, louder this time.

I snapped to attention. "Oops, sorry," I said.

"Have you solved the problem on the board?"

"Um . . . ," I stalled. I couldn't believe I'd been caught daydreaming in math again. I squinted at the board. None of the numbers made any sense to me.

Then, from the corner of my eye, I saw Felicia turn her notebook toward me. She kept her eyes on the front of the room, but I could see the answer.

"Fifty-one point four?" I answered.

Mr. Reid nodded. "Very good," he said. "I hope you do as well on our quiz next week."

Phew! That was close.

After class, I went over to thank Felicia for helping me. I figured I should apologize to her about our conversation at the shelter on Tuesday, too.

But Arielle was waiting for Felicia at the door. She grabbed Felicia's arm and whispered something in her ear, and then they both walked away, giggling down the hall.

So much for apologizing.

I got to the locker room early.

So this was it. Final cuts. I put on my old green-and-yellow AYSO uniform for luck.

"Hi," the girl next to me said. Her soccer jersey had *Larsen* printed on the back. "Traci, right? Good luck out there today."

"Thanks," I said. "You too."

The girl smiled. "I'm already on the team," she said. "I'm just here for practice. My name's Lydia, by the way."

"Nice to meet you," I said.

"Hey, aren't you and Amanda Kepner running that All For Paws fund-raiser on Saturday?" Lydia asked.

I glanced over my shoulder. Arielle was sitting a few benches away, tying her cleats.

"Yeah," I said. "We're hoping a lot of people will show up. It's a really good cause."

"I'd like to go," Lydia said. "But I'm probably going to Arielle's party. Most of the team is, I think." She stretched her arms out and swung them back and forth. "Well, guess I'd better hit the field. See ya."

I dropped onto the bench. It sounded like most of the school was going to Arielle's instead of the fund-raiser. Bummer.

I looked over at Arielle again, but she was gone. I stood up. I had to get onto the field, too.

When I got there, it seemed like all the girls around me were wearing blue and white. And a lot of people had come to watch, too.

My mom was there. And Dave. Amanda and Felicia. Even Ryan was there, standing with his brother.

I guess soccer tryouts were a big deal here in

Wonder Lake. It was almost like a real game.

Arielle was already warming up, spiking the ball off her head and dribbling with her knees.

"Way to go, Arielle!" someone called from the sidelines.

What a show-off.

Coach Talbot gave a sharp blast on her whistle. "Let's go, ladies!" she shouted. "We don't have all day."

We ran over and Coach Talbot gave us instructions for a new drill. It was harder than most of the ones from Wednesday. Each girl had to get through five eighth-grade defenders to the goal. And they were all pretty tough.

After a few more drills, Coach Talbot divided us into teams again for another scrimmage.

This time Arielle got a yellow jersey and I didn't. Was that good or bad? Maybe it didn't mean anything.

The scrimmage started off okay. For me, anyway. I made my first goal.

"Way to go, Traci!" I heard my mom shout.

Coach Talbot called a time-out. She wanted to talk to Assistant Coach Ferris about something.

I glanced back at Arielle. She was bent over at the waist, breathing hard.

When Coach Talbot started her stopwatch again, one of my teammates passed me the ball. Arielle ran straight at me, her green eyes glinting.

But suddenly, she stumbled. Catching herself, she turned to look back at Coach Talbot. Big mistake. In that split second, a defender plowed into her from behind.

Arielle hit the ground. The defender took the ball and passed it back upfield to me. I dribbled the ball all the way to the goal and kicked it in.

Piece of cake.

Arielle was back in the game a second later. But she seemed to be falling apart.

For the rest of the scrimmage, she barely came near the ball; she kept stumbling, and she missed a couple of easy passes.

I made two more goals, but Arielle didn't make any. I could hear the crowd murmuring, and they were all wondering the same thing I was:

What was the matter with Arielle Davis?

Coach Talbot called us off the field so two more groups could scrimmage.

Arielle headed slowly toward the sidelines and sat down in the grass. She didn't say anything to anyone.

Something was definitely wrong.

"Arielle, are you okay?" I asked, sitting down next to her.

"I'm fine," she said. But her eyes were filled with tears.

"Come on, Arielle, what is it?" I said.

Arielle looked around to make sure no one was

listening.

"Look, I blew it, okay?" she said. "I got a little nervous. That's all. It happens to me sometimes." A tear escaped down her cheek and she quickly brushed it away. "No big deal."

"Maybe you should talk to Coach Talbot," I said. "I'm sure she'll understand."

"No!" Arielle said. "It's too embarrassing."

"No, it isn't," I said. "You could just—"

Arielle bit her lip. "I probably shouldn't even have told you that," she said. "You're supposed to be my competition. But you've definitely made center forward now."

"Not necessarily," I said. But I knew Arielle was probably right. I'd done pretty well out there today. And she hadn't.

We didn't scrimmage again. I guess Coach Talbot had already made up her mind.

As I left the field, Amanda and Felicia and Ryan all waved to me. Then my mom came running up. "You were terrific, Traci!" she said, giving me a big hug.

Ordinarily, I would have been mortified. But it was nice that she'd come down to the field to see me play. Even though making the team might keep me from being in orchestra.

"Thanks, Mom," I said.

"Let's go straight to the Ice Cream Emporium to celebrate," she said. "Whether you make the team or not. You played like a star. That's what's important."

I rolled my eyes. Why did she always treat me like a little kid? "No thanks, Mom," I said.

"Hey, you may not want ice cream, but *I* do," Dave said, coming up behind us. "I'm starving. Let's go."

Just then, I saw Arielle walking up the hill to the locker room all by herself. She didn't look like the Arielle I knew at all. She seemed really sad and lonely.

"Mom, can you wait here just a second?" I asked.

I ran back onto the field. Coach Talbot was making some final notes on her clipboard.

"Um, Coach Talbot?" I said. "Could I talk to you for a minute?"

The coach frowned and rubbed her sunburned nose. "What is it, Traci? I need to get this list up soon."

I hesitated. "Well, I'm not sure how to say this. I mean, maybe I didn't make center forward. But if I did, and Arielle didn't, I think she should get it."

Coach Talbot looked confused. "Excuse me?"

"Well, see, I won't have time to play every game. I'm in the orchestra, and I help out at an animal shelter after school," I rushed on. "Soccer means so much to Arielle. So I was thinking, maybe I could be the *relief* center forward."

"I think I'm the one to decide who is the best player for each position," Coach Talbot said sternly.

"But Arielle *is* the better player for center forward. She was just having an off day today. And since I'm so busy . . ."

Coach Talbot didn't answer right away. She tapped her clipboard with her pen. "I still don't understand why you're doing this, McClintic," she said. "But I'll think about it. Why don't you go hit the showers?"

"Okay, Coach," I said. "Thanks."

I ran back to join my mom and Dave. I didn't need to stick around to see who'd made the cuts. Everything was going to work out. I just had a feeling.

chapter
FOURTEEN

FROM THE DESK OF ARIELLE DAVIS
TO DO:

Call EVERYONE!!
Talk to DJ—sound system?
Buy colored lights
Cancel manicure
Hot dogs/hamburgers—pizza?
Felicia's mom: cupcakes, brownies, cookies
Sodas/chips (& lots of water!): ask Dad to pick up
games/sports stuff
Get new outfit

AMANDA L. KEPNER
TO DO:

CALL MORE PEOPLE!!!
SOUND SYSTEM—NEED MUSIC?
DECORATE PET VAN?
HOT DOGS/HAMBURGERS (SAL—PIZZA
COUPONS?)
FELICIA'S MOM—BAKED GOODS. STILL OK?
TENNIS BALLS, FRISBEES, SMALL ANIMAL TOYS
PRINT OUT RAFFLE TICKETS—TRACI
SODA, WATER (TONS!)

"No, thanks," another kid told us. It was Friday afternoon. Amanda and I were handing out more All For Paws fliers near the entrance to the school library.

We didn't have many takers. Most kids probably already had a flier. Or they just weren't interested.

Inside the library, Arielle and Felicia were sitting at a table, their heads together, talking and scribbling on a piece of paper. The door swung open and Felicia looked up at me, but the second she caught me looking at her she turned away, giggling.

"So what's up with Arielle and Felicia?" I asked Amanda. "Is it just me, or have the two of them been acting weirder than usual?"

Amanda nodded. "Arielle's been completely avoiding me," she said. "And I have no idea why."

"I thought you guys made up on Sunday," I said.

"I thought so, too." Amanda shrugged. "She didn't even seem that psyched about making the soccer team. Maybe she and Felicia are just busy planning the party. Tomorrow's the big day, remember?"

"I haven't talked to Felicia much, either," I said. "I thought everything was okay between us, but she keeps running off with Arielle every time I see her."

Another kid walking into the library shook his head when Amanda tried to hand him a flier.

"Okay, that's it," she said. "I give up. I don't think we can hand out any more of these."

"I guess everyone's going to Arielle's party," I said

with a sigh. "Maybe we should ask Mr. Fiol if he needs any last-minute help."

But when Amanda and I called Felicia's dad from the school pay phone a little while later, he said he had everything under control.

"Are you sure?" I asked him.

"Absolutely," Mr. Fiol said. "See you girls tomorrow at one o'clock."

"But that's too late," I said into the phone. "The fund-raiser *starts* at one o'clock."

"No problem," Mr. Fiol said. "I have some volunteers setting up. You girls have done enough already, believe me."

"Well, okay," I said doubtfully. "Thanks." Then I hung up.

"I guess we should just go home and relax tonight," Amanda said.

"I don't think I'm going to sleep much," I said. "I'm way too nervous. What if no one shows up for the fund-raiser at all?"

Amanda grinned. "Hey," she said. "Remember what our homeroom teacher always says?"

I smiled back. "Positive attitude?"

"Right," Amanda said.

I was trying. I really was.

By the time one o'clock rolled around on Saturday, both Amanda and I were pacing around my living room. Amanda had arrived at noon, dressed in jeans and a "Save the Manatees" T-shirt.

Dave was sprawled out on the couch, giving the remote control a workout. Even *he* didn't say much, which was unusual for him. All of us were waiting for Mr. Fiol to arrive.

"I guess the whole school must be getting ready for Arielle's party by now," I said glumly.

Just then, the doorbell rang. "Hello, hello!" Mr. Fiol called in a jolly tone. "Ready to go?"

"At least *he* doesn't sound worried," I said to Amanda as we went out the door.

Mr. Fiol had driven his van. But the only animal inside was Lola.

"Hey, cutie-pie!" I greeted her.

Lola danced around the back of the van. She seemed really excited to see us.

"Where are all the other animals?" Amanda asked.

"Oh, they're down at the green already," Mr. Fiol said. "Don't worry, everything's been taken care of."

"Move over, Squirt." Dave squeezed into the van beside me, as far from Lola as possible. He was starting to sneeze already.

Mr. Fiol drove to the center of town and pulled into a spot just off the green. I snapped on Lola's leash. Then we all walked to the fund-raiser together.

"I can't look," Amanda said, covering her eyes. "Is anyone there?"

Mr. Fiol chuckled. "Look and see."

I couldn't believe it. The green was packed with people and animals! Music was blaring from the bandstand.

Then we saw the sign: PARTY FOR A GREAT CAUSE: ALL FOR PAWS! ADMISSION $3.

I almost fell over in shock. Felicia and Arielle were sitting under the sign—taking tickets!

"Party?" I said. "What's going on?"

Amanda and I looked at each other. Then it dawned on us. Arielle was having her party here—at the fund-raiser!

When Arielle and Felicia saw us, they got up and came running over.

"We wanted to surprise you," Felicia said breathlessly. "You *are* surprised, aren't you?"

"Totally," Amanda said.

I just nodded, speechless.

There were streamers around the bandstand and lampposts. And little colored lights in the trees, for when it got dark. The whole green was dotted with booths and areas marked out for the animals to play.

"Cool," Dave said.

I turned back to Felicia. She was wearing a white jeans skirt and a pretty flowered halter. I gave my friend a huge hug. "Felicia, this is amazing," I told her.

"Isn't it great?" she said, beaming. "Can you believe how many people showed up?"

I shook my head. "Where did they all come from?"

Felicia grinned at her dad. "Well, I talked Dad and Arielle into combining the fund-raiser with her party. It totally made sense. And then we called up everyone who was invited to Arielle's party and told them to come here instead."

"So that's why you guys have been whispering and avoiding us the last couple of days?" Amanda said.

"Sorry," Felicia told her. "But we really wanted this to be a surprise."

"Um, Traci, can I talk to you for a minute?" Arielle asked me in a low voice. "In private?"

I shrugged. "Sure."

Uh-oh, I thought. *What does she want?*

Arielle led me over to a picnic bench set up under a tree. She looked great in dark jeans, a cool red halter top, and matching red sandals. Her toenails were painted red, too.

I couldn't help wishing I'd dressed up a bit more. I was wearing plain old jeans and a white T-shirt. I thought I'd just be hanging out with the animals all day. I didn't know I was going to a party.

"Look, Traci, I know we haven't been getting along that well," Arielle began.

I had to give her credit. She got right to the point.

"But I wanted to thank you for talking to Coach Talbot," Arielle continued.

My mouth dropped open. "How did you know?"

"Coach Talbot told me," Arielle said. "You didn't have to do that. But thanks."

I kicked at a pebble in the grass. "Well, you'll make a great center forward," I said.

Arielle flipped her hair back. "I know," she said, and smiled. Same old Arielle.

"Thanks for moving your party," I told her.

"Oh, that was all Felicia's idea," Arielle said. "You know, that girl may be quiet—but once she gets an idea into her head she never shuts up."

I glanced back over my shoulder. Felicia was standing near the bunny races with Amanda. Next to them, Ryan was choosing a rabbit to enter in the race.

A bunch of kids came over then to talk to Arielle. One of the girls was holding a big orange tomcat. "Isn't he cute?" she said. "I've already named him Sylvester."

"Well, I'm ready to party," Arielle said. "There's dancing over by the bandstand. Let's go."

"I think I'll just hang out for a while," I told her. "I'll see you later."

"Whatever," Arielle said, shrugging. "Have a good time today, McClintic," she added over her shoulder, as she walked away with her friends.

"You know I will," I called back.

"Hey, can you hold this crazy dog while I go get a burger?" Dave asked me. Lola seemed to be walking *him* rather than the other way around.

"No problem," I said, taking Lola's leash. Dave headed off toward one of the grills run by the Wonder Lake Fire Department. Lola tugged hard on her leash, trying to follow him.

"Easy, girl," I said, scratching her ears. "You have to behave yourself today."

The music from the bandstand was getting louder, and somewhere behind me, a loudspeaker crackled. "The drawing for the fifty-fifty raffle will be held tonight at seven o'clock," a voice said. "Buy your tickets at the gazebo. Remember, the more you buy, the more you can win. All to benefit the Wonder Lake Animal Shelter."

Lola kept tugging at her leash. "What's the matter, girl?" I asked her.

"Hey, Dixie Chick." Ryan Bradley was standing beside me wearing wraparound shades and a bright purple T-shirt.

"Um, hi," I said. For some reason, I felt myself blushing a little. Ryan seemed different outside of school. More easygoing or something.

"You know, that's my dog you've got there," he told me.

"What?" I was so surprised I almost dropped Lola's leash.

Ryan reached down and ruffled the St. Bernard's fur. "Yup. I told my dad about Lola and he said we could adopt her. We've been thinking about getting a dog for a while. And she's a pretty cool dog."

I gulped. "She sure is."

"I bought her a collar over at one of the booths," Ryan said. He pulled a bright red collar from his pocket. It even had rhinestones, just like the one I'd drawn.

"Well, if I can't have her, I'm glad you'll be her owner," I said.

I felt like I was going to cry. But I wasn't sure if I was happy or sad.

"Hey, I live right down the street from you, remember?" Ryan said. "You can visit her anytime."

"Thanks," I said. "That'd be great."

"Want to go dance?" Ryan asked. "A lot of kids from school are over at the bandstand."

"But what about Lola?" I asked. She was wagging her tail and jumping all over Ryan.

Ryan shrugged. "We'll take her with us. Come on!"

As the three of us headed toward the bandstand I couldn't stop smiling. This was the best day I'd had since I'd moved to Wonder Lake.

"Over here, you guys!" Amanda called to us.

Ryan, Lola, and I pushed our way through the crowd of dancers. Felicia, Arielle, and Amanda were dancing together, waving their arms in the air and acting silly.

Ryan and I started dancing with them, too, with Lola wagging her tail and panting between us.

"Hey," I shouted to Amanda over the music. "I wanted to ask you something."

"What?" she shouted back.

"Where *is* Wonder Lake, anyway?"

At that exact moment, the music stopped.

Amanda, Felicia, Arielle, and Ryan all burst out laughing. "Should I tell her?" Amanda said.

"Sorry, folks," the DJ called. "We're having technical difficulties. But we'll get the tunes back on soon."

"Traci," Amanda said, smiling, "I hate to break this to you. There *is* no Wonder Lake."

My mouth dropped open. "What do you mean, no lake? You're kidding, right?"

"No," Amanda said. "Sorry. It's kind of a town joke."

I turned to Arielle. "But you told me it was near my house."

Arielle shrugged. "Well, sort of," she said. "Your street ran along what used to be the lake. They drained it a long time ago for a housing development."

"Oh," I said. I couldn't help feeling a little disappointed.

"Hey, Dixie Chick, don't take it so hard," Ryan told me with a grin. "There's another lake nearby. We can take Lola there sometime."

"We can all go," Felicia said.

"We could even go tomorrow," Arielle added.

"We have a minivan. I'll ask my dad to give us a ride," Amanda said.

Right then, the music came on, and everyone started

dancing again. Lola jumped up and put her paws on Ryan's stomach. I guess she wanted to dance, too.

Felicia grabbed my right hand and Amanda grabbed my left. Then Arielle linked hands with them, and the four of us made a circle, laughing and swaying our hips to the beat.

The music was loud, and the air smelled like burgers and cotton candy. I squeezed my friends' hands and thrust my hips to the side. I was really getting into it.